George Cockburn

John Chinaman

His Ways and Notions

George Cockburn

John Chinaman
His Ways and Notions

ISBN/EAN: 9783337166731

Printed in Europe, USA, Canada, Australia, Japan

Cover: Foto ©Raphael Reischuk / pixelio.de

More available books at **www.hansebooks.com**

JOHN CHINAMAN

PRINTED BY TURNBULL AND SPEARS

FOR

J. GARDNER HITT, 37 GEORGE STREET, EDINBURGH.

LONDON: MARSHALL BROTHERS, 10 PATERNOSTER ROW.

GLASGOW: JOHN SMITH AND SON, 19 RENFIELD STREET.

JOHN CHINAMAN

HIS WAYS AND NOTIONS

BY

Rev. G. COCKBURN, M.A.

FORMERLY OF ICHANG

Edinburgh

J. GARDNER HITT, 37 GEORGE STREET

1896

To

WM. L. BUCHANAN, Esq.,

MERCHANT IN GLASGOW

THIS BOOK IS DEDICATED BY THE AUTHOR

" To produce and to nourish, to produce and have not, to act and expect not, to enlarge and cut not off—this is called sublime virtue."—LAO-TSE.

PREFACE

ANOTHER book on China demands a word of explanation. The writer does not flatter himself that he is possessed of keener vision than others, but he may have looked from a somewhat different standpoint. The attempt is to portray the representative man of the people and not to deal technically or exhaustively with things Chinese. All the author claims is sufficient opportunity of observation, whether he has used it well or ill.

NEW DEER, 2nd Feb. 1896.

CONTENTS

CHAPTER I

CHAPTER II

CHAPTER III

9

CONTENTS

CHAPTER VII

CHAPTER VIII

CHAPTER I

PRIMITIVE SURVIVALS

The Typical Chinaman — Fetichism — Charms — Coercing the Deities — Totemism — The Dragon — Animal Folk-Lore — Changelings—Naturalism—The Supreme Ruler—Heaven and Earth—Astrology—Lucky Days—The *Fung-shui*—Luck in Counters and Sign-boards—Worship of the Dead—Hungry Ghosts—Graves—Coffins—Burial of the Poor—Conveying the Ghost—A Letter to the Devil—Burning the Demons.

THE typical Chinaman is a man of the lower middle class; a master tradesman, a small shop-keeper, or a farmer. Law-abiding and thrifty, sober and industrious, his virtues are homely and of home growth, but they wear well. In no country, perhaps, is there a larger propor-tion of the people above the condition of day-labourers and yet compelled to practise fru-gality and work hard for their daily bread. Mandarins and Emperors may come and go, but the ordinary Chinaman holds on the even tenor of his way. It is to him that I would

introduce the reader.   He has many good qualities and a host of prejudices, the guiding
principle of his life being to walk in the old
paths. He is redolent of the native soil, and in
this age of folk-lore and place-literature deserves
not to be overlooked.   He is a relic of primeval
times, and to primeval times we must go if we
would understand his notions and his ways.

Fetichism, which is the lowest stage of human
thought and religious belief, has left many
traces in China.   Sacred trees, fountains and
stones, to which the natives devote paltry offerings, are abundant—more numerous, in fact,
than most residents suppose.   These objects are
not considered to be divinities, nor even the
abode of spirits.   The Chinese say they are *ling*,
i.e., possessed of some mystic potency; but as
they do not formulate their belief in clear-cut
creeds and dogmas, it is very difficult to get anything from them that is sufficiently definite to the
Western mind.   It is enough for them that these
things are *ling*, and that the worship, or whatever
we may term it, is an ancient custom in the

locality. The average Chinaman feels no call to explain or to defend it ; he laughs at its absurdity when you begin to talk with him, and inwardly marvels at the foreigner's curiosity ; for his own part, things must have come to a pretty pass if he must rack his brains before complying with an old custom which is the reverse of onerous.

Closely allied to the foregoing is the universal use of charms. One of the most potent is a stone from the *Tai Shan*, Great Mountain. The Tai Shan is celebrated in legend ; and it is firmly believed that neither demon, ghost, nor evil influence will come near a stone from the famous hill. But neither good spirits nor bad are supposed to know everything. A wide-awake Chinaman will always undertake to cheat the devil ; and he seldom troubles to procure a stone from the veritable mountain, when he can get a likely block at the nearest quarry. A board will do, or even a piece of the brick wall plastered. If there be anything by the door-post bearing the inscription in large characters, " This is a stone from the Tai Shan," no bad luck nor unearthly

visitors will invade his dwelling. The mere sight
of it is like brandishing a whip before slaves; but
how beings so stupid as not to distinguish a stick
from a stone should be credited with ability to
read the crabbedest of all orthography is a large
question. A Chinaman's answer is the familiar
and all sufficient "old custom." My own con-
jecture is that it is of a piece with the sentiment
of my old teacher, that I might well shorten our
hours of study, as I should know the language
well enough when I had consumed a sufficient
quantity of China rice and water. Unless the
literary attainments of the demons are to be
credited to the climate, the problem must be
given up. My pundit's plea for less work was
not altogether a pretence. Some Chinese ladies
were visiting my wife when I called out something in English, and one of them asked our
native nurse what it meant. She replied that she
did not know. "Not know! How long have
you been here?" "Two years." "You have
eaten the foreigners' rice for two years, and you
do not understand their talk!"

Wormwood and sedge are in as much repute as rowan tree and woodbine formerly were in our own country for a similar purpose. Indeed, if we accept Sir John Lubbock's definition of Fetichism as "that stage of religious thought in which man supposes he can force the deities to comply with his desires," almost the whole of Chinese religion is still in this stage. In times of drought or excessive rain the image of the god who presides over the weather is taken from the temple and set outside that he may know how he has been mixing up the seasons, and get a taste of the miserable effects of his own negligence. If a man's favourite domestic deity proves unpropitious, he has no scruple in using the image to boil his kettle, throwing it on the dunghill, or taking it to the pawnshop. One sometimes overhears a worshipper in the temples, at the close of his devotions, tell the divinity that if he does not show more favour, he will receive no more incense, candles, and prostrations.

The dragon is the grand totem of the country;

B

and with the partial exception of the dragon, no animal, real or supposititious, is worshipped by the Chinese. The Imperial dragon has five claws, and no subject is permitted to represent the monster with more than four. He has no wings, but rides on the wind and pours down floods upon the earth. Other dragons inhabit the earth and the deep. The Emperor sits on the dragon throne, and the national ensign is the dragon flag.

Caves are the peculiar haunt of the dragon, especially those containing springs or pools. Every district has its cave, sacred to the dragon king, where pilgrimages are made in times of drought. On these occasions, a lizard caught in the cave is frequently put in a jar and worshipped as the representative of the dragon king. At other times the pilgrims content themselves with worshipping the images of the gods which are in the cave, it being generally converted into a sort of temple. If the drought is very great, the district magistrate may have to go in sackcloth and sandals to fetch water from the sacred pool, which is carried to the district city and poured out with much ceremony.

The dragon may be over-active as well as too remiss. Some time ago the Ichang magistrate put out proclamations that the *Chiao*, the dragon of floods, was to visit the locality, and disaster could only be avoided by scaring him away. To effect this, the peasants were advised to dig deep pits in the earth, as if they intended to capture the creature.

The *lin*, often called the unicorn, is a huge monster, half-dog, half-tiger, covered with scales. It is supposed to devour avaricious and incompetent officials : and has not appeared of late years. The *fung-whang*, or phoenix, is always represented as a bird of the pheasant tribe.

The tortoise, the hare, and the fox are reckoned uncanny creatures, and few care to kill a dog. Amongst the lower orders there is little prejudice against canine flesh, which may always be had in the market under the name of earth mutton, but a right-minded Chinaman does not like to shorten the days of an animal which once did meritorious service. At the time of the flood, of which they have many stories—how far original and how far derived from Mahometan and Christian sources, it is impossible to say—a dog, which had been shut out of the ark, swam after it with a few ears of rice sticking to his tail. The Chinaman feels gratitude for the preservation of his favourite cereal.

Many will not eat beef, and others avoid it unless certified that the animal has died a natural death. This is not due to religious prejudice, but arises from the sentiment that the animal which ploughs the fields should not be brought to the shambles. Our own aversion to horse flesh must have arisen in the same way, as it was eaten by our ancestors, and our prejudice against it cannot well spring from the Mosaic Law, or our scruples would have extended to the pig, the hare, and the oyster.

The swallow and the bat are lucky animals, and a mandarin feels flattered when he is likened to a wild goose. The monkey is the emblem of stupidity and perverseness. Its physical endowment is excellent, but in the wild state it shows no remarkable instinct, and when domesticated, learns neither good manners nor useful work. The lizard is poisonous, and is possessed of the evil eye. A well-known story relates how several members of a family took successively ill and died with all the symptoms of poisoning. The mandarin was informed, and came to make investigations on the spot. It turned out that all had been seized after eating millet pottage made by the daughter-in-law, and the circumstantial evidence was strong against her. Still the mandarin hesitated to pronounce sentence, and had an idea there was something in the case no witness had brought forward. The woman was ordered to make a mess of pottage in the mandarin's presence the same as before. As the savoury odour filled the house the eagle eye of the official saw a lizard creep from a cranny in the roof and gaze fixedly into the cauldron. The whole mystery of death in the pot was explained, and an innocent woman acquitted.

The souls of animals, as well as evil spirits, often

enter the body of young children. Chang Chi-tung, Viceroy of Nanking, is reputed to be animated by the soul of a monkey, which was kept as a pet in his paternal home and dis-appeared about the time of his birth. His Excellency bears several marks on his body similar to those on the monkey, and proof posi-tive is found in his personal habits, which are decidedly simian. The great man never bathes and seldom washes—at the best, a Chinaman's ablutions consist in rubbing himself down with a damp cloth. The Viceroy never changes his underclothes, but puts on an upper garment to repair the waste underneath. He never undresses, and seldom goes to bed, but doubles himself up in his arm chair for a nap at odd moments. With all this he enjoys the best of health, and his activity is incessant. Report has it that he is well acquainted with the story himself, and by no means resents it.

Plants and their properties receive a due share of attention, but the stories connected with them are neither so numerous nor so interesting. A twig of the peach tree figures prominently in magic, and Confucius himself believed that the future might be divined by the leaves of the trefoil. The bamboo seeds in years of famine, and the chrysanthemum is the emblem of wedded love because it blooms in autumn.

Our typical Chinaman is full of these quaint stories and old world notions, and seldom fails to forecast the fortunes of the day from the first sight or sound of the morning. One of the most unlucky things is to hear a monkey hooting, or the sound of the gongs as a prisoner is being led to execution, before tasting food. But enough has probably been said on the whole subject.

What may be termed Naturalism is the primitive cult of China. The worship of the spirits of wind, rain, clouds, water, mountains, land, and grain, is lost in the mists of antiquity, and is still observed at an altar of earth outside the South Gate of a city by the mandarin of the place. The god of land and grain is worshipped by farmers, and the god of thunder, who may, however, be modern, with the beak of a bird and armed with a mallet, is held in universal awe. Otherwise this ancient cult has fallen greatly into decadence, pushed aside by later deities of more pronounced personality.

Alongside of these nature gods, the Chinese worshipped Shang-ti, the Supreme Ruler; but there is no record of a time when he was regarded as the sole deity. The old notices are confused and dim, and it must be remembered that we possess these documents only in the form in which they have been transmitted by the Confucian school. They were honest transmitters, but they complain that their materials were fragmentary and uncertain. It becomes a nice question to determine how far the received text is tinged by the opinions of the editors. As they stand, the old documents would lead us to suppose that the worship of Heaven and Earth is as old as the worship of Shang-ti. Anciently, as at the present day, some Chinese regarded Heaven and Earth in a material way, and some not. Confucius uses Heaven and Earth as the equivalent of Shang-ti. Is the identification older than his day? No man could put his ideas in clearer language when he wished, but Confucius was a statesman—a pity he lived before Parliament and the Caucus, for his language upon these points is so delightfully ambiguous that there are two sections among the Sinologues, one holding that the sage believed in a personal God, and the other that he did not. A two-fold tendency probably existed in China from an early time, one to identify Shang-ti with Heaven and Earth, the other to limit the worship of the Supreme Being to the supreme man, the Emperor. Primitive monotheism has partly degenerated into blank materialism, and partly become crystallized in the gorgeous ritual of Imperial worship. It has long ceased to be a living force. Still, one hears the peasants speak in a reverent way of *Tien Lao-yeh*, the Mandarin of Heaven, but they offer him no worship. Every Chinaman, however, worships Heaven and Earth. Scholars may be metaphysical in their explanations, but there is no evading the fact that the typical man of the people is a thorough-going materialist. At the best, Chinese ideas of God are eminently unsatisfactory, but such as they are, no possible ingenuity can evolve them from Chinese Naturalism; nor has any hypothesis been suggested that will bear inspection, but the view that they are the fading rays of a clearer light, which they did not like to retain in their knowledge.

As might be supposed, astronomy plays an important part in things Chinese, but nothing to the rôle assigned it among Aryan nations. The Chinaman has his myths, but he sets his heroes to drain the marshes of the Yellow River, instead of chasing each other round the zodiac and playing hide-and-seek with the revolving seasons. The summer and winter solstices are special times of Imperial worship, and the new and full moon are seasons of sanctity. The month is lunar, and on the first and fifteenth people leave off work an hour or two earlier, and expect a flesh dinner. The most careless then pay their respects to their ancestors, and hang a lantern outside their doors at night. Moon cakes are eaten on the fifteenth of the eighth moon, but the sun and moon are not worshipped, and the popular star gods are of Taoist origin, forming no part of the original nature worship.

Astrology is believed in as a matter of course and of ancient custom, nor will the typical Chinaman commence any undertaking without consulting the Imperial Almanac for a lucky day. This is an official publication compiled by a board at Peking, closely resembling Zadkiel and Old Moore. Private enterprise in almanac making is strictly forbidden—a wise provision, for were there no standard authority to refer to in the matter of lucky days, business would be at a dead lock.

Other influences besides the stars are perceived to have a bearing upon mundane affairs, and the Chinese philosopher has his own ideas about causality. He takes for granted that the whole universe is permeated with subtle essences, and swarms with supernatural beings. The question is, how to secure the good and escape the bad.

The science of the *fung-shui* decides that, by
diagnoses and prescriptions too intricate for the
ordinary man ; but there are numerous professors
whose skill may be commanded upon reasonable
terms.   My old teacher was a noted expert and
firm believer in the art, and took great pains to
instruct me in its principles, on telling him that
the science was unknown in my own country.
The brilliant and benevolent idea occurred to the
old man of initiating me into the mysteries of
luck, and he felt assured, if I would return to my
ancestral home and put his lessons into practice,
I should attain to great prosperity in a land
where people went about their business in a hap-
hazard manner.

Fung-shui literally means wind and water, and
to the uninitiated barbarian seems simple enough,
but to the inhabitant of the Flowery Land it is
a name to conjure with.   Good and vivifying
influences and benignant spirits come from the
sunny South; for the sun is *yang*, the active
principle in nature.   Bad influences come from
the North ; and the East is generally better than

the West. The science rests on an astronomical basis, and a compass with astrological and cabalistic signs is used to lay down the bearings. But it soon leaves the heavens and becomes of the earth earthy. Everything may be upset by the configuration of the land, the course of running water, surrounding buildings, the prevailing winds, or conspicuous objects in the distance. The first thing is to discover the veins of the earth, in determining which the above are the chief factors. The most fortunate spot of all is termed the dragon's pulse ; but after you have secured it, all may be spoiled by your neighbour building an addition to his house or digging a well, to intercept your luck below or your benign influences above. In a Chinese law court obstruction of the *fung-shui* is as good a plea as blocking an ancient light or cutting off a water supply among ourselves. A Chinaman tells you he does not like splitting the heavens and riving the earth. Opposition to railways, steam engines, factories, and foreign-built houses are invariably founded on the *fung-shui*. Quite recently a mine was ordered to be closed because it would interfere with the imperial graves about fifty miles distant, disturb the repose of former emperors, and imperil the present dynasty. Another savant attributes the calamities of his country to the sacred characters of his language being painted on tea boxes, and, he is credibly informed, irreverently trodden under barbarian feet across the sea. The theory that Tenterden Steeple was the cause of the Goodwin Sands is an excellent instance of the *fung-shui*, and it was fairly matched three years ago by the natives of Shanghai, who declared that the bad condition of the Woosung Bar was due to the new tower that had been built on the English Cathedral. During my residence in Ichang, the natives spent upwards of £3000 building a temple on the top of a hill overlooking the city, as the best means of improving local industries. The object was to make the roof of this temple higher than the top of a neighbouring hill from which the influences were bad. Near the same place is another hill with the shoulder of it cut away by a wealthy family to improve the luck of their ancestral burying-place.

To secure a lucky spot for a grave, a dwelling-house, or a place of business, is as essential as to commence upon an auspicious day; but should the *fung-shui* be bad, improvement is not hopeless. A useful device, very much employed, is to build a blank wall a few yards before the door. This serves as a barrier against the demons, whilst there is a way round the end for benign influences. Much depends on how the walls of the house stand to the points of the compass, the mountain tops, and the adjacent streams. If placed at the right angle, the good will come to stay and the bad will fly off at a tangent. Very often it is enough to put up a charm or paint a devil's head facing the obnoxious quarter, and one sometimes sees the plaster model of a cannon mounted on the roof to keep unearthly visitors at bay. Neither disease nor remedy, however, is likely to be discovered by an amateur. When there is prolonged sickness or other misfortune in his home, it is as natural for a Chinaman to consult the professor of luck as it is for us to call the doctor and inspect the drains. A simple remedy usually puts all to rights, but when there is a European in the case nothing will do but to pull down his house, by a riot if need be. The mandarins profess themselves to be utterly powerless, but when they have any project of their own in hand, it is marvellous how easily the populace is appeased and danger averted. The *fung-shui* never prevented a battery being built and armed with Krupp guns ; nor had the Viceroy at Wuchang insurmountable difficulty with his cotton factory and iron works with steam tramways and tall stalks. Yet, should the Viceroy lose his head, as is quite possible one of these days, the man in the street will put it all down to his tampering with the *fung-shui*, and it is very questionable if the official class be one whit more enlightened than the plebeians.

A shopkeeper often imagines his success to be bound up with his old counter. The native banker with whom I did business was a thriving man and made no secret of this opinion, taking in good part any chaff about his counter being patched until it had lost its identity, or the need of moving into larger premises to meet the requirements of his trade. I had the good fortune to be considered by him a lucky person to have dealings with, having, for my own convenience it must be confessed, persuaded him to deal in exchanges on the foreign banks at Hankow and Shanghai. The business grew in his hands, and proved lucrative. In purchasing some property for the Mission, over £200 had suddenly to be paid down to complete the bargain. Several weeks would elapse before I could procure an order on a foreign bank, and in my difficulty I turned to my friend the native banker. He at once advanced the money, charged no interest, and would accept neither security nor even my written acknowledgment of the sum advanced.

In the palmy days of Hankow, before the British housewife had developed a taste for Indian tea, one of our clansmen flourished as storekeeper at the Port. An observant native marked his luck, and came to the conclusion

that it was associated with his sign-board.
When the Scotsman retired, the Chinaman got
hold of his sign, put it on his own store, and
proclaiming to all the world that his name was
Macgregor, did business and prospered in his
turn. When last I passed through the street
I looked for the emblem of clan Alpine, but
it had apparently succumbed to the tooth of
time.

When a Chinaman imagines that the luck is
with him, he usually succeeds; and as every
traveller speedily discovers, when his boatmen
or his coolies are decidedly against moving on
or making a halt, it is wise to let them take
their own way. To a certainty their fears will
bring their fulfilment.

A lucky spot and a lucky day are desiderata
at all times, but absolute essentials for the interment of the dead. The other world is a
shadowy, cheerless place, and the welfare of
the departed largely depends on the services
rendered them by the living. There must be

a decent funeral on a lucky day, and the grave must be in a spot where the *fung-shui* is good. But the departed always require more than that, and the full ritual of ancestral worship claims the sanction of Confucius, who pronounced the characteristic maxim, " Serve the dead as you would serve the living." Not easy to comply with, but the representative Chinaman does his best, and those few who may differ from him in their opinions are very careful to conform to him in their practice. Twice a year, at least, food and drink are offered to the spirits of an-cestors; and on these occasions piles of paper money and paper clothes, miniature houses and representations of all the necessaries of life, paper sedan chairs and paper bearers, paper opium, pipes, and lamps, the implements of gambling and the requisites of pleasure, everything which could conduce to the comfort of the dead, judging by their predilections when alive—all are burnt with appropriate ceremonies, and filial piety has no misgivings that the transparent shams are transmitted as ghostly realities to the right parties in the land of shades. The most miserable of all fates is to wander in Hades as a hungry ghost; and there is nothing else in store for those who leave no male descendants to minister to their wants. Chinese philanthropy largely takes the form of ministering to the hungry ghosts. On what may be called All Souls' Day, troops of Buddhist and Taoist priests are hired to say mass for their repose; mountains of paper money and clothes are burnt for the benefit of indigent spectres; and at night myriads of small paper lamps are lighted and sent floating down the Yangtse River to light the spirits of the drowned on their way to Sheol. When the feast is over, a Chinaman no longer hears the shrieking of unhappy sprites in the howling of the night wind, and dreads neither blight upon his crops nor murrain on his cattle.

With all its puerility there is much in Ancestral Worship that appeals to right feeling, and it is impossible not to see in it a blind groping for something to worship, nearer than the dim and distant Supreme Ruler, and more human than the impersonation of rain and storm. A man's own ancestors are the beings in the spiritual world most near at hand and most ready to help. Their names are engraved on the ancestral tablet, which is the most sacred of a Chinaman's penates. On all occasions of importance he prostrates himself before this tablet, and with burning incense and lighted candles presents the sacrifice of food and drink. Twice a year ancestors are also worshipped at the graves, and the graves repaired. This is usually made the excuse for a family picnic, and is one of the rare occasions on which a Chinese woman may enjoy a day in the open air. There is a meal *al fresco*, and as the household returns in the afternoon it is felt that they can hold up their heads with the best, having duly celebrated their ancestral rites and fixed a bunch of white paper streamers upon the graves to bear testimony to the fact.

There are no graveyards, and an old grave is never opened for a fresh interment. Graves

occur everywhere except inside city walls. For
miles in the neighbourhood of a town the hills are
thickly studded with the abodes of the dead ; but
in the fields and by the wayside the symbols of
mortality are ever present. Only on the change
of a dynasty may graves be levelled, and when
the present Manchus came to the throne they
made it a special act of grace not to insist upon
it.   As might be supposed, no inconsiderable
portion of the country is given over to the dead,
but fortunately the luckiest situation for a grave
is on high or rising ground, the places least valuable for cultivation.   A hole is made in the
ground, sufficient to admit the coffin, and a mound
like a haycock is heaped above it. Sometimes,
in damp places especially, the coffin is placed on
the surface and built over with bricks, plastered
and white-washed. People provide their funeral
requirements before death, and the most esteemed
gift a dutiful son can give to an aged parent is a
handsome and substantial coffin. It is carried
through the streets with flags and music, and received with the greatest pleasure. The chief

corner of the best apartment in the house is assigned to it, and one seldom enters a Chinese drawing-room, or guest hall, without finding several coffins in it. Nor are they always empty. The funeral may be delayed for years, waiting for a lucky day, or until the purchase of a lucky spot for a grave can be effected, for absent members of the family to return, for money to perform the obsequies with appropriate *éclat*, or for convenient means of transporting the body to the family resting-place in a distant part of the empire. The coffin is made of expensive wood several inches thick, often a foot, lined inside with chunam made of lime and wood oil, hard as stone, and well coated outside with the excellent native varnish, of a dark colour. The body, dressed in the finest clothes, is packed with quicklime, and, objectionable as it seems to have the mouldering remains of humanity in a room occupied by the living, it is very rarely that the faintest odour can be detected.

All Chinese cannot be buried in this fashion. The poor are placed in a rough shell of old boards, and laid side by side, as close as they will pack, in the public burying-ground, and covered in the scantiest manner with mother earth. The public burying-ground is often utterly inadequate, and coffins are piled above each other in a huge heap, and bodies in all stages of decomposition are devoured by dogs and kites. In other cases the coffin is abandoned by the wayside, or left to moulder on the hills. Children are seldom buried with any ceremony, but wrapped in a piece of matting and thrown without the gates, or consigned to the baby tower, a round building without a door, but with several openings in the wall to admit the bodies, which is conspicuous in most populous places.

In conclusion, it may be noted that Ancestral Worship, although not idolatry in the strict sense, is irreconcilable with any system of monotheism, and, apart from the puerility of much of it, is incompatible with progress. A man feels himself as much bound to the ways of his forefathers as he is attached to their person. All innovation is unfilial. The typical Chinaman may admit that your plans are feasible, but he finds heresy and schism in driving a cart when his grandfather wheeled a barrow. Confucius denounces those who worship their ancestors and yet presume to innovate on their plans.

At funerals a white cock is placed on the coffin to convey the soul from the house to the grave. The mourners wear white sackcloth, and when their means can afford it, there is a long procession with banners, a howling company of professional mourning women, and bands of priests in full canonicals chanting prayers, burning incense, beating drums and gongs, and firing crackers. As soon as life is extinct, a priest is employed to write a letter to the devil, giving the deceased a good character. When several children die successively in a family, they imagine there is some demon with a grudge against them who is entering their children and spiriting them away. The only way of putting a stop to the calamity is to take the child as soon as it expires, or even while it still draws breath, to make sure the demon has not escaped,

and burn its body to ashes. This is done outside among the graves. The child is placed in
a rough coffin and set on a pile of firewood.
They carry out the child unobservedly to the
graves, and as soon as the sticks are lighted
run off. Whether they imagine that they burn
up the evil spirit, or only give it a blaze to
frighten it, I could never ascertain. It is an
"old custom," and, as they believe, a sure cure
for infant mortality, and they enquire no further.

CHAPTER II

SCHOOLS AND SCHOOLMASTERS

Education Appreciated—The School and the Teacher—Method
of Teaching—Nature of the Language—Course of Study—
Higher Education—Confucius—His Philosophy—His Politics
—Shih Whang-ti—The Sphere of Women—Confucius on
Religion—The Old Philosopher—Evolution.

THE schoolmaster is abroad in China. "Rear
pigs and not children," says the proverb, "if you
do not educate them." But there is no system
of national schools, nor compulsory attendance,
education being so highly prized that the need
for these is not felt. It is a thing unheard of in
Central China for a person, who can afford it, to
allow his boys to play the truant or remain un-
taught. All but the very poorest can there read
and write, but in some districts, more especially
in the South, book learning is not so common.

There are Government and endowed academies
for students preparing for the literary examinations, but elementary schools are all private ad-

ventures, taught by candidates who have failed at the examinations, or graduates who are poor and have not secured Government appointments. The school is a room in a dwelling-house, a mud cabin, or a mat shed, where twenty or thirty scholars are collected, each bringing his own desk. The teacher is at his desk seven days in the week, and his labours commence at dawn and finish at dusk. The bamboo rod is much in evidence, for "in teaching without rigour the schoolmaster is at fault." The work is hard and the remuneration poor enough, ten or twelve shillings a year from each scholar, seldom more than the wages of a day labourer, but no man in the community is more highly honoured than the teacher.

The same books are used in all schools, and the scholar commits them to memory. The literary language differs from the colloquial, and the pupil has made considerable progress in reading and writing before the meaning of a single character is explained. There are no home lessons, and the scholars are not taught in classes. Each one goes up with his book to the master, and has a sentence read to him ; he then returns to his seat, where he repeats the words over and over at the top of his voice, swinging his body to and fro to assist the memory. In due course he returns to the master's desk, wheels round, " backs the book," in scholastic phrase, and shouts out what he has learned in a stentorian chant. The noise is agonizing, and the monotony of memorizing is varied only by lessons in writing, in which the Chinese use a small brush and China ink ground and mixed on a small slab as required. No other branches are taught at school.

Secondary education consists in reading the commentaries and mastering the details of the Confucian Classics. Couplets are composed in a very artificial measure, and essays written in a stilted and antiquated style upon themes selected from the works of the sage. But there is neither grammar, rhetoric nor logic, for the Chinese language and ratiocination withstand all attempts to be reduced to rule. The same word, written and pronounced in the same way, may usually be a noun, a verb, or an adjective, even a preposition or conjunction, according to its position in the sentence, and arbitrary usage. The position of words counts for much, but Chinese is pre-eminently a language of fixed phrases. Certain principles may be discovered, but exceptions are so numerous that there is no sure guide but a knowledge of the use and wont in each case. The language is monosyllabic, and the sounds are remarkably few. In the Mandarin dialect all syllables are open, or end in a nasal *n* or *ng*. The number of separate vocables is under 500, but as each word is pronounced with a certain fixed tone, a Chinese ear can distinguish more than 1000 different sounds. There are four fundamental tones, but they are liable to be sub-divided, and in this way they amount in some dialects to as many as eight. The tone is not an accent, but comes near a musical note. Even with this device to eke out the paucity of sounds, the number of symphonous words is extremely great: *cp.* dear, deer; you, yew, ewe. Ambiguity in speaking is usually avoided by reduplication, as we might say sheep ewe, tree yew. There is no inflection. It is surprising in how many cases the context is a sufficient guide, and where more is needed separate words are employed for number, gender, voice, and tense. There is no alphabet, each word having its own distinctive mark or character; but there are 214 radicals, one or other of which must enter into each character, unless it be itself one of the radicals. The form of a character is little guide even to a scholar either to sound or sense, and in different parts of China the characters are pronounced very differently. In the South-East the number of dialects, mutually unintelligible, is very great; but in the rest of China some sort of Mandarin is spoken. Although they cannot talk to each other, people all write the same character. They read it differently, but the meaning is as plain to all as the multiplication table to the various nations of Europe. With the Chinese character already in existence, the invention of Volopuk seems a work of supererogation. The written language is extremely terse, whilst the spoken is very diffuse. This terseness would be sacrificed by any system of alphabetic or phonetic writing, and the one language of the empire would become a group of tongues as different as the various forms of Teutonic speech. These drawbacks, together with their innate conservatism, have induced the Chinese to cling to their hieroglyphics although they have known about alphabetic writing for ages. A Chinaman will never allow that the indication of a sound can be as definite and expressive as the symbol of a thing.

The geography, history, and laws of China are acquired in studying the classics, whilst no information about foreign languages and nations or Natural Science is deemed worthy of attention. Arithmetic is learned in the counting-house by those who pursue a mercantile career. In making computations they use an abacus with two beads on the upper portion of the wire and five on the lower. Their money, weights, and measures are all decimal, except that there are 16 ounces in a Chinese pound (lbs. 1⅓ Avoir.).

The universal primer is the San-tse-King, Three Character Classic, a jingling metrical conglomeration in lines of three syllables. It opens with the statement that man's nature is good, but his practice will be defective if he grows up uneducated. "If you do not learn when you are young, what will you do when you are old?" It enumerates the elements— fire, earth, wood, water, metal, the sorts of grain cultivated, and the animals reared for food. It gives the dynasties that have reigned in China, and anecdotes of sundry worthies, not forgetting old Mung's mother (the mother of Mencius), who had much trouble in finding a place of dwelling in which her young son would not be con-taminated by vile surroundings. The object of the book is to serve as an introduction to the Confucian Classics. After the primer comes a dry list of Chinese surnames, and perhaps the Two Thousand Character Classic, two thousand different characters strung metrically together without a single repetition, and, as may be supposed, with very little rhyme or reason. Having digested these light brochures, and "backed the book" without mispronouncing or omitting a single syllable, the aspirant to literary distinction attacks in turn the Great Learning, the Doctrine of the Mean, the Analects of Confucius, and the Memorabilia of Mencius. These are the Four Books, and a common school education seldom goes much beyond this stage. An ordinary workman can often repeat the whole of them from memory, which appears to outsiders to be the only faculty that is much cultivated; but for memory no European comes near a Chinaman. The natives, however, value education because it familiarizes the young idea with the "rejuvenating doctrines" of the national sage.

After the "Four Books" come the Five *King* or Classics; Spring and Autumn (a historical chronicle written by Confucius), the Book of Ceremonies, the Book of History, the Book of Poetry (ancient ballads), and the I-King, or Book of Changes. This last is believed to contain the sum of all wisdom, but the Chinese confess that the key to it has been lost in these degenerate times.   European sinologues mostly consider it a very fragmentary and obscure work on divination and fortune-telling.   It is the oldest of Chinese books.   The received text is faulty, and there are no materials extant for a satisfactory revision.

From the hedge school to the Forest of Pencils there is no variation in the above curriculum. Education begins and ends with Confucius, and an idea of what the scholars really do learn may best be gathered from a short account of the sage.

Confucius was born in the state of Lu, in the modern province of Shantung, in the year B.C. 551, and died B.C. 479.   His father was a military officer who married a second time late in life, and although his lineage is traced to the ancient kings of China, the family was in decayed circumstances.   China was then divided into a number of petty states under a feeble hegemony, and Confucius spent his life in the service of various princelings. He shifted from court to court, but could find no one to brook so upright a minister and so severe a monitor. He was often an outcast, and in the direst poverty refused to accept place or presents from those he considered tyrants ; but did not scruple to tell a lie when it would serve his turn. In retirement he taught a school or academy, and had seventy favourite disciples. His life was a sad one, for which it is evident he had largely himself to blame, and we should form a lower estimate of the man did we not know the enthusiasm and devotion he inspired in those who knew him best. His son was little better than a fool, but his grandson inherited no small portion of the temper and ability of the sage. His descendants are still numerous, and the head of the family enjoys the only hereditary patent of nobility in China proper. He divorced his wife and died defeated, among his last words being the verse of an ancient ballad :—

> "The great mountain must crumble ;
> The strong beam must break ;
> And the wise man wither away like a plant."

He was tall and of a commanding presence, of a swarthy complexion, austere and of few words, punctilious in dress and manners, and apparently his sole relaxation was to accompany his voice upon the lute. His disciples relate that he was particular about clothes and food. In entering a room he would not tread on the doorstep. " He required his sleeping dress to be half as long again as his body." " The fur robe of his undress was long, with the right sleeve short." " He did not eat meat that was not properly cut, nor what was served without the proper sauce, nor anything that was not in season." " He took a little ginger after his meals." He ate sparingly and according to measure, but drank wine (beer or whisky?) according to his natural thirst. To such-like minutiæ his disciples attach as much importance as to weightier matters.

" No intelligent monarch arises ; there is not one in the Empire that will make me his master. My time has come to die." Such was his lament when he felt his end approaching ; and certain remarks show that he had very little, if any, hope beyond the grave. But no sooner was he dead than Duke Gae exclaimed, "There is none now to assist me on the throne," and caused a temple to be built, where he offered sacrifice to the sage. In the year B.C. 194 the Emperor visited his tomb and sacrificed an ox. Henceforth honours have been showered upon his memory, and by none more than the present Manchu occupants of the throne. In every Chinese city there is a temple to Confucius, where the officials have to offer stated worship. There is no image in it, only a memorial tablet, and other tablets to his most famous followers. The worship is the same as that paid to the gods, but Confucius is not regarded as a god but as a perfect man. Over the gate of his temple is inscribed, "Equal to Heaven and Earth." He is "the one man of ten thousand ages," and in every Chinese school the scholar must bend to the tablet of Confucius before taking his seat.

The greatest thing about him is his personality, and the way he has stamped it upon the nation. Confucius is the ideal Chinaman, just as "John

Bull" is the ideal Englishman. In worshipping him they are offering incense to themselves. He wrote little, but his conversation has been recorded by his disciples. He collected and re-edited the ancient literature of China. He was a "transmitter and not a maker." He repudiates being the author of what he taught. Considerable portions of what are loosely called the Confucian Classics were written by subsequent generations of scholars, and the canon closes with the Memorabilia of Mencius, B.C. 372-289. The inspiration claimed for this heterogeneous pile is that it was written or sanctioned by sages who natually embodied the right way. Confucius, however, claims no more for himself than to be a diligent student of antiquity and a lover of the old paths, which are in accordance with the principles of Heaven and Earth—laws of nature come as near his meaning as any idea familiar to us.

His philosophy is moral and political, the *summum bonum* being the Empire brought to a state of happy tranquillity. There is no attempt to construct a psychology, but the axiom is laid

down that man's nature is radically good, and
nothing is required but good examples and the
dissemination of right principles. These are " dis-
played in the records." The five cardinal virtues
are benevolence, uprightness of mind, propriety
of demeanour, knowledge, and good faith. The
five prime relationships are between sovereign
and subject, father and son, elder brother and
younger, husband and wife, friend and friend.
" Filial piety and fraternal submission are the
root of all benevolent action." But Confucius
says nothing of the duty of parents to their
children, and it is quite in accordance with his
principles that there is no law in China against
infanticide. In popular tracts the kindness of
parents is always represented as pure benevolence
to their children, and no argument is adduced to
stimulate parental care beyond pointing out that
children ill brought up will neither reverence their
parents when alive nor worship them with the
proper ceremonies when dead. Whatever their
age, children are in abject subjection to their
parents. They must yield implicit obedience,

and can hold no property which the father may not claim.

Confucius states the golden rule in its obverse form. "What you do not like when done to yourself do not do to others." This is "the compass and the square" for measuring human conduct. Stated merely as a prohibition, it falls far short of the Gospel precept. " Recompense injury with justice, and recompense kindness with kindness." He leaves very little room for repentance. "You cannot carve in a rotten stick." "If you sin against Heaven, you have nowhere to pray to," but the sense of sin is very indistinct. In the Chinese language there is but one word, *tsui*, both for sin and crime. It means also a mistake or a breach of etiquette, and very often amounts to no more than our conventional phrase, " Beg your pardon." ·This indistinctness is a very accurate reflection of the Confucian teaching.

In politics Confucius had nothing better to recommend than benevolent despotism ; but he was no preacher of passive obedience. He justifies the deposition of bad rulers, and condemns the infliction of punishment where there has been no instruction ; but he did not rise to what we would call national education. He dreamt of princes searching out the worthy to bear rule, and they would be guides and fathers to the people, who would bend to their benignant sway "like corn to the breeze." He considered it would be as easy to make a nation happy as "to look on the back of your hand." The country was torn by civil strife, yet he accepted the feudal system as destined to go on for ever, and could only hope for intelligent princes to arise, and propose' such rose-water cures for disorder as returning to the old court cere-monies. He is great upon etiquette and the right use of names. But he is not quite so absurd as a Westerner may suppose, for to the Oriental mind there is much in a name and a form. Still, it was not Confucius who tran-quillised China, but the greatest enemy of his system who has ever arisen. Shih Whang-ti, B.C. 221, the Prince of Tsun, in Western China, attaining the chief power, became actual Emperor instead of suzerain. He abolished feudalism and established the present plan of government by graded officials holding office for a fixed term. His line soon came to an end, and Confucianism regained ascendancy, but it made no attempt to undo the work of the reformer. It was Shih Whang-ti who burnt the Confucian books with the exception of the I-king, which he probably considered too obscure to be unsettling. His memory is held in loathing by the Chinese, who re-echo the sentiments of the Confucianists which they are taught at school, but his name deserves to be better known than it is as the only statesman who ever framed a constitution which has endured for more than two and twenty centuries. There will be another burning of the books, or its equivalent, when China comes to its awakening.

The vision of Confucius was bounded by the "Four Seas" which enclosed the "Middle Kingdom." Only the "black-haired people" were capable of improvement. The "outer barbarians" are to be governed by "misrule." These

principles have brought his followers much grief
since they came in contact with European
Powers.

The Master had a poor opinion of woman.
Her sphere is the home and the family. She
should attend to the kitchen and the nursery,
but should know nothing of the outer world or
her husband's affairs. He sets down the dis-
tempers of his time very largely to husbands
listening to their wives' advice, and expressly
states that it is the greatest depravity for a man
to leave his father and his mother and cleave
to his wife. A woman is allowed no standing
in the eye of the law. Not only does Confucius
assign to her a subordinate position, but he does
not suppose she would profit by a school education. He sets her down as being essentially of
an inferior nature, and in no sense a help-meet
for man. He says there are very few women
who are not jealous, but the unfortunate illus-
tration he adduces is the usually ill-concealed
chagrin of the wife who finds herself supplanted
by a handmaid in the affections of her lord.

Under all circumstances his will should be her pleasure. Confucius says he found "girls and servants the most difficult persons to behave to," and we can well believe him.

He says nothing of a future life or judgment to come, but rests his system on a purely secular and utilitarian basis. But in this life the way of transgressors is not invariably so hard, nor is virtue so evidently its own reward as to render a morality which takes account of no higher considerations very binding in actual practice. He accepted, or at least he did not openly dispute, the primitive ideas spoken of in the last chapter. He warned his disciples not to offend the prejudices of the vulgar; but at the same time he asked them, "If you cannot serve men how can you serve the gods?" He would not speak of monstrosities, feats of strength, or the gods. The category is his own, and is sufficiently indicative of his attitude. He prefers to use the impersonal term Heaven to the name Shang-ti. He says Heaven is intelligent, but, like his followers at the present day, he appears to have some conception of an intelligent principle or law which is not conjoined with personality. He insists on the worship of ancestors, and probably believed in ghosts, which subsist for a time after death and gradually become dissipated. This is the professed belief of his disciples at present. They often justify their worship of the sage by saying that his personality was so strong as not yet to have become defunct. In all Confucian writings spirit means no more than an attenuated form of matter, or an ethereal emanation from it.

It is not correct to say that Confucianism, whilst not strictly speaking a religion, supplies the place of religion to those who profess it. It does no such thing. Confucianism never saved a single Chinaman from the silliest superstition. Explain and minimize it as we may, every Chinese, the mandarin as much as the coolie, worships Buddhist and Taoist idols ; and this idolatry they all confess Confucius does not sanction, and is contrary to the whole spirit of his system. Religion is put in the background, but there is nothing supplied that either satisfies or supplants the religious instinct.

It is just possible for a European to turn Mahometan or Buddhist ; no one but a Chinaman ever professed to be a Confucianist. A millennium in the past, no future at all, and nothing better to do for the present than return to the primitive institutions of Yao and Shun and the duke Chow, do not beget enthusiasm in the Western mind. The sage has given his countrymen a good conceit of themselves, but his utilitarian teaching has not made them true patriots. He has, however, made them ultra-conservatives, with the rooted conviction that every change is a change for the worse. But Chinese conservatism has a good many planks of the platform of British radicalism. Confucius is hard on capitalists and the non-productive classes. He is against hereditary legislators, believes in the nationalisation of the land, and holds that each family should be possessed of five hens and a pig.

The fifth century B.C. was prolific in sages, and

China had more than one. But of the life of Lao-tse, the Old Philosopher, by which designation he is generally known, there is almost nothing authentic. He is said to have been named Li, and to have been keeper of the records at the Court of Chow. He is the acknowledged head of the Taoists, but his system has little in common with the vagaries of that sect. Of his writings we possess only a small treatise, about the size of St Mark's Gospel, upon *tao*. There is great diversity of opinion as to what he meant by the term, which may be translated, *way, reason, doctrine, word*. The best native commentaries prefer way, a road that may be walked in.

There is an apocryphal story that the two wise men once met. Lao-tse could see no good in digging up the "rotten bones" of antiquity, and the man of ancient ceremonies confessed that he had met a dragon who mounted on the wind and soared through the clouds to heaven. The dialogue is a late invention, but Livy himself puts no more appropriate speeches in the mouths of his heroes. Confucius is much among the "rotten bones," and Lao-tse very often in the clouds.

The opening sentence of the *Tao-teh-king* is a good specimen. "The Way (*tao*) that may be *wayed* (*tao*, as a verb,) is not the eternal way. The name which can be named is not the eternal name. Non-existence is named the antecedent of heaven and earth; and existence is named the mother of all things." "Existence and non-existence mutually originate each other." "These two are one and the same." "The Way is all-pervading." "The Way is ever inactive; and yet leaves nothing undone." "The Way produced unity; unity produced duality; duality produced trinity; and trinity produced all things." "The great thing is to lay hold of the Way, by non-action, meditation, and introspection." "By non-action there is nothing that may not be done. One might undertake the government of the world without ever taking any trouble."

He supposed the Way to have existed before God, and like Confucius he had no conception of spirit but as an attenuated form of matter.

E

But Lao-tse was no mere dreamer. Confucius laid down the rule, "If the scholarly man be not grave, he will not call forth any veneration, and his learning will not be solid," to which the old philosopher retorts, "If some men would but abandon their sageness, and cast away their wisdom, the people would be benefitted a hundred fold." In direct opposition to the Master he recommends to "recompense injury with kindness." Confucius could not see that wisdom and virtue might accomplish their ends without being joined with power in the state, but Lao-tse exhorts his disciples: "Find your great in what is little, and your many in the few." "Water is good to benefit all things; while it does not strive, but runs to the place which all men disdain. Inasmuch as it does not strive no one dislikes it." "To produce and to nourish, to produce and have not, to act and expect not, to enlarge and cut not off—this is called sublime virtue." "The sage is the good Saviour of men. He rejects none." "The bad men are the material of the good men." Very different sentiments these from those of Confucius, who dismissed unapt scholars and would not "carve in a rotten stick."

The treatise of Lao-tse is not canonical, and the student who applied it in his essay at the public examinations to establish any doctrine would doubtless secure a blank mark, still it is included in an authoritative list of books to be read for example of life and instruction of manners.

Both systems accept material evolution and are based on the same cosmology. In the beginning was Chaos, the absolute, the limitless, the great extreme. In process of time arose the *yang* and *ying*, the active and passive principles, symbolised as light and darkness, male and female, motion and rest. By action and interaction, ebb and flow, these two produced the universe as we now see it. Heaven and earth, gods and men, animals and plants, and the five elements, things seen and unseen, are all the products of the same evolving forces. Intelligence, the Tao (Way), or Li (Principle) is absolute; but personality or self - consciousness

arises from the "great abyss" as the product of
development. Often have I heard an educated
Chinaman maintain that it was utterly repugnant
to his mind that personality could precede matter
or the material universe be created by spirit, but
he had no difficulty in conceiving spirit and consciousness to be evolved from matter.

CHAPTER III

THE THREE RELIGIONS

Nature of the Gods—Want of Reverence—Introduction of Buddhism—Failure of its Philosophy—Buddhist Temples—The Priesthood—Stipends—Mass—Trustees of Temples—Prayers in an Unknown Tongue—Heaven and Hell—The Ritual—Salvation by Works—Merit and Demerit—Moral Results—Resemblance to Romanism—Taoism—The Taoist Clergy—The Taoist Pope—Spiritualism—Exorcism—The Temple and the Stage—Sectaries and Mahometans—Latitudinarianism.

WITH such a theory of the universe, the Chinaman believes none of his gods to be omnipotent, omniscient, or eternal. They are unseen beings, very much to be dreaded, because his knowledge of them is very uncertain, but it does not follow that it is impossible to deceive them or to bend them to his will. As to their moral nature, many are bad, some are good, and most, like man himself, are a mixture of the two. Like the *moira* of the old Greeks, there is a power behind the gods.

When taxed with levity and want of reverence, the Chinaman replies that his worship is

good enough for the beings it is offered to ; and
when inconsistencies and contradictions are
pointed out, he has the ready answer that there
are many rival powers and conflicting interests in
the *yang kien*, the world of sight, and he supposes
it must be the same in the *ying kien*, the world of
shade or spirit. He is very sensitive to a personal insult, but he bears you no ill-will because
you are a heretic, and laughingly tells you that
neither you nor he knows anything for certain.
Very possibly all parties are right : why should
there not be as many rival pantheons as there are
rival nations ? For his own part, what was good
enough for his father is good enough for him.
Further discussion is needless, for that time at
any rate.

How the Chinaman became possessed of his
patchwork of a religion may be clearly traced
and is far from having received the attention it
deserves. When Confucianism succeeded in
placing an insurmountable barrier between the
common people and the Supreme Ruler, it supplied nothing that could satisfy their religious

cravings; even patriotism which has sometimes taken the place of religion was a thing only for kings and rulers. The common people had only Heaven and Earth—the material heavens and earth they would be to them—and the ghosts of their ancestors left. Their souls could not live by these and their daily toil. Men were bound to ask the questions upon which Confucius had refused to speak, and it was India that gave an answer.

The received account is that the Emperor Mingti had a dream in the year 65 A.D. that a sage had appeared in the West, and despatched an embassy to bring reliable accounts of his teaching. In the mountains of Thibet his emissaries turned southward and came in contact with Buddhism on the banks of the Ganges. They returned to China with three Hindoo priests, a few Sanscrit books, and some relics of Buddha. This was the introduction of idolatry into China, and gods more human than the Chinese had known. The Brahminic revival in India sent crowds of Hindoo priests to China. As many as three thousand laboured in the country as missionaries at one time, but it was long before the new faith obtained a firm footing.

As a philosophy Buddhism failed to carry any of the positions of Confucius, and gradually settled down, if we may use the figure, in the territory which the master had not made his own. The Confucianists attacked its morality and not its credentials. The celibacy of the priests, their claim to peculiar sanctity, the turning of men's thoughts from the affairs of life, were specially obnoxious. But Buddhism touched true chords in the human heart. On the future life it gave forth no uncertain sound; it presented gods with human sympathies; it held out hope to those who were defeated in this life; it dazzled the populace with gorgeous ceremonies; it had austerities for the devout and the self-denying; it sold indulgences to those who preferred religion by proxy. The Chinese accepted transmigration, but they are not usually strong believers in its extreme form. Yet all admit the *lun whei*, the revolving wheel, by which retribution is awarded for the deeds done in the body.

Buddhist temples abound everywhere. They are filled with images of the living, in marked distinction to the temples of Confucius which contain only the memorials of the dead. The idea is that of a school. The lesser gods are arranged in rows along the sides of a hall listening to the instructions of Buddha who is seated on a throne at the upper end. The doctrine of the Nirvana took little hold on China, and has been superseded by a sensual paradise called the Western Heaven. I have examined hundreds of Buddhist temples in Central China, but never came across but one devotee who was sitting in contemplation in anticipation of annihilation. The Nirvana is not, however, strictly annihilation, but a state of which nothing can be predicated, neither being nor not-being, absorption in the great abyss.

There are three grades of divinities :—Fuh (Buddha), the enlightened ; Lohan (Arhan), those who have conquered evil passions ; Pusah (Bodhisattwa), those who adopt Buddhist doctrines with great vigour. The chief Buddha is Shakyamuni, an Indian prince. His highest title is *Ju-lai*, he who comes (from nowhere and goes nowhere). Amida Buddha, O-mi-to-fuh, Buddha of the boundless age, is more popular in China. O-mi-to-fuh is muttered as a prayer and ejaculated as an oath. Instead of a bad road being mended, these mystic syllables are often engraven upon the rock where the path is particularly dangerous. The Lohans, eighteen in number, sixteen Hindoos and two Chinese, are very little worshipped, but ornaments are often made with small figures of the Lohans and worn as charms. The Pusahs are countless in number, and being supposed to retain no small portion of ordinary human feeling, are the most worshipped of all. So much so, that Pusah is the colloquial term for a god of any kind ; but it would be considered a great insult to call Confucius a Pusah.

The only professed followers of Buddhism are the priests. All others say they are followers of the three religions, Confucianism, Buddhism, and Taoism ; or profess to call no one master but the national sage. The priests call themselves *seng*, members of assembly, but their common designation is *hosang*, a name of very doubtful origin and significance. They are celibates and live under monastic rule, dropping their family name. They do not worship their ancestors, and, of course, have no descendants. Hence no one likes his son to become a priest; and although some who are weary of life seek the seclusion of a monastery and others become monks to gain an easy living, the ranks of the priesthood are mainly recruited by children bought with temple funds from poor parents. They shave their heads quite bare, and if the priest be fully ordained, there are nine small round scars above his forehead left by the burning of the moxa at his consecration. They wear a peculiar dress, but it is seldom of the sacred yellow; and not one in ten is a strict vegetarian, as demanded by the Buddhist creed. Their ceremonial robes are gorgeously embroidered, but their large images are of clay and the smaller of wood, made without art, and decked with paint and tinsel. Very few temples contain any articles of value, and such as they have they are always willing to sell to the European collector of curios.

Some temples have large endowments, but the income from this source is inadequate to maintain the crowd of priests. A few solicit alms, going through the streets with bowl and wallet, beating the " wooden fish," an instrument shaped like a human skull, but their chief means of livelihood is the offerings of worshippers at the temples, and most of all fees for saying mass. On the occasion of a death, no one, not even the strictest of Confucianists, neglects to have priestly prayers said for the dead. This is done at the house of the departed; inside the house if sufficiently large, otherwise in the street before the door. The priests bring their ceremonial robes, missals, drums, and images at nightfall. A table is arrayed with idols, lighted candles, burning incense, and sacred utensils. Round it the priests howl their prayers in monotonous intonation, varying the proceedings with genu-flexions and twistings of the fingers to an accompaniment of crackers, drums, and gongs. If sufficient money be forthcoming this goes on till gray dawn, and the amount that can be squeezed out of the family decides the number of times which the ceremony has to be repeated to get the soul out of purgatory. Filial sons pay handsomely for the repose of a father or a mother, but the saying of mass by Buddhist and Taoist priests detracts in no way from the necessity of observing the primitive ancestral rites. These have been overlapped but not superseded by Buddhism.

A few temples are the property of individual wealthy families, but generally they are built by subscription and managed by the people of the district. Some are entirely in the hands of the resident priests, but whoever may act as trustees, the civil power is always ready to step in to prevent abuses. Occasionally a temple is demolished by the mob when the priests are notoriously scandalous. Chinese do not like their women to frequent the temples; and I have seen official proclamations posted at the door of certain temples, warning the people not to allow their wives and daughters to go there. These the priests dare not tear down.

Buddhist prayers are in Sanscrit, the sounds being represented as nearly as possible by Chinese characters. The knowledge of Sanscrit is altogether obsolete among Chinese priests—I never could hear of one who pretended even to know the letters—and they have gone on for ages repeating their prayers mechanically in an unknown tongue from these transliterations. Heaven and hell are peopled with divinities, graded according to the model of the Chinese government, and they have made no scruple of admitting to their temples many idols of Taoist origin. The early Buddhists were great preachers, but the practice has fallen into complete desuetude. Now-a-days the priest does nothing except for ready money. There is no Sunday, and no social worship. Chinese Buddhism is selfish and disintegrating. When a man goes to worship, it is usually to ask the favour of some deity in his undertakings, or to enquire what luck will attend him. The priest rings a bell to attract the attention of the god, usually fires a cracker to keep off evil spirits, who cannot stand the smell of gunpowder, lights two candles and three sticks of incense, intones a prayer, and hands the lots to the worshipper, who knocks his head on the ground and casts them. If unfavourable he tries again, probably turning to another image, or going to a rival temple.

Salvation by works is the unchanging nucleus of the protean forms of this religion. There are no beings in the spirit world so powerful as mortal men who have obtained freedom from desire by their own merits. Every action brings its own reward. The wheel must continue to turn until every sentient being becomes a Buddha and passes into the Nirvana. The ordinary Chinaman is in no hurry about such a consummation, but contents himself with aiming at the Western Heaven, or such modicum of merit as will prevent his being next born a woman or inferior animal. The repetition of prayers, acts of worship, and deeds of charity are all valuable means of accumulating merit. Merit is transferable, and the priest has always on hand a large stock from his works of supererogation, which he is prepared to part with for a consideration. When he can find customers he conducts a sort of spiritual exchange, giving for ready money bills payable on demand in the other world. Any sin may be compounded for by a corresponding merit. All that is needed is to keep the balance on the right side. There are lists of all conceivable actions with the amount of their merit and demerit accurately appraised. Rightly expended, a small sum will cover a multitude of sins.

This idea has taken an enormous hold on the Chinese. A street beggar never asks alms, but calls on the passers by to embrace the opportunity of accumulating merit. Merit is readily acquired by saving life. A favourite method is to buy a jar full of shrimps, which are brought to market alive, and empty them in the river. Buddhism has done something to inculcate kindness to animals, but it has done a great deal by weakening the barriers between man and the lower animals to bring about that callousness to

the sanctity of human life which is so marked a
feature of the far East.   It has taught self-denial
for a selfish end, and must be held largely responsible for the ingratitude from which their best
friends cannot acquit the Chinese as a race.   Still
Buddhism is very far from being destitute of good.
It has kept a future life and future retribution before the Chinese.   It has taught them patience
under suffering, and, in its own way, charity to all
men.

The resemblance of Buddhism to Roman
Catholicism has been often pointed out.   The
Jesuit fathers declared it to be a caricature of the
Mother Church devised by the enemy of man.
The rosary, the pastoral staff, prayers in an unknown tongue, mass for the dead, adoration of
saints and relics, images with glories round their
head, the celibacy and tonsure of the clergy, incense, bells, candles, the exorcism of evil spirits,
abstaining from meats, the selling of indulgences,
monastic rules, and vows of poverty, are common
to both systems.   Both affect a dim religious light
in their places of worship, intone their prayers,

F

pronounce the benediction with only the three front fingers extended, have priestly vestments, and consider priestly services to be an *opus operatum*, very much independent both of the worshipper and the celebrant, so long as the latter is properly ordained and goes through the prescribed forms. Possibly they derive their ritual from the same source, but what would really interest the student of human nature and the devout Christian would be the elucidation of those longings in the human heart that call forth priestcraft, mystery, and ritualism.

Buddhism, even in its Chinese development, is largely metaphysical. Taoism rests on another foundation. Laotse himself would have treated religion and ethics as branches of Natural Science. The eternal way is not discoverable, but in casting about for a way that men may walk in, he came very near the position of modern science. He formulated no complete system, and left his followers to carry out his principles in their own way. They became recluses dreaming of a corporeal immortality, pursuing researches into alchemy and astrology. Their great object was the composition of the golden pill, or elixir of life. The rise of Buddhism compelled them to organize in self-defence. They borrowed the ritual and ceremonies of their opponents, and fought them with their own weapons. But they adhered to materialism. The soul is, as it were, an essence, distilled in the alembic of discipline of the body. It is not the spirit, but the body that is to be purged of dross. Their gods are appropriate to a religion based on materialism. The stars are divine: magicians, hermits, warriors, popular heroes, all have a place in the pantheon. The god of literature, the gods of diseases, the god of wealth, the god of the kitchen, belong to Taoism. It appropriated the old nature gods, reproduced the Supreme Ruler as the Gemmy Ruler, embraced dragons, genii, the phœnix and other supernatural creatures. It took the *fung-shui* as specially its own, and became learned in luck and fortune telling. In its temples, it attempts to surround the gods with the glories of paradise. It is a darker superstition than Buddhism, and does its best to supply the ordinary Chinaman with a religion that will be in accord with his natural desires.

There are two classes of priests, monks and secular clergy. The former live in monasteries under rules similar to the Buddhists, the latter marry and live in their own houses, holding licenses from the Taoist Pope. This personage, styled the Teacher of Heaven, lives in the Province of Ngan-whui, and is a descendant of Chang Tao-ling, a famous magician, who lived about the time of our Saviour. He is recognised by the emperor, and holds rank as a high official, being supposed to hold all the demons under his control.

The Taoist priest is ready to say mass for the dead or perform any ceremony of the Buddhists, but his chief business lies in spells and charms. They employ sleight of hand, and possess some knowledge of chemistry, optics and other branches of natural science. A Buddhist priest is ready to show everything and tell everything, but the Taoist keeps back much from the European. Their temples are open and there is no difficulty about their ordinary worship, but their seances which take place at night are not readily to be observed with the care that one could wish. Their mediums, apparently in a state of trance, their muscles rigid and their eyes starting from the sockets, give forth utterances which are taken as the voice of the god. They resent investigation, and at private seances to which an unbeliever would not be admitted the natives report table turning, writing on the sand by a suspended twig of peach tree, and the appearance of bodies floating in the air. The Taoist priest can point out a thief, lay a ghost, charm away an ague, and secure a fair wind or a good bargain. He can fix a small mirror above the door of a house to keep away the devil, who turns in terror when he sees his own likeness, or like another St Patrick, he will write a charm to drive away the bugs and fleas. No native house is without it, but I can testify it is a fraud.

Buddhist and Taoist priests never enter into

controversy with each other, and, hold little
intercourse. Although they have many ceremonies and gods in common they do not join
in their worship. Occasionally they are to be
seen in each other's temples on a friendly visit.
Taoist priests wear the old national dress of
China, and put the hair up in a top-knot. The
pig-tail and ordinary Chinese dress were introduced by the Manchus.

The temples of both sects are externally alike,
and the inside arrangement, in reality distinct,
seems much the same to a cursory visitor. There
is no fixed day of worship. The door is always
open, and anyone may enter. The European
gives no offence by examining and handling
everything and asking questions. In one corner
will be a pleasure party at dinner, in another a
group of idlers gossipping with the priests, or a
company of gamblers intent upon their play. A
temple is always provided with a stage, and does
duty as a theatre. The profession of an actor
is accounted disreputable, but the pieces represented, although seldom edifying, are not as

a rule specially objectionable. The performance is by daylight, and the plays are of such intolerable length that they run on for days. The audience has to stand, but no one remains for the whole piece, the connection being so loose that it is unnecessary. There is no scenery, but the get-up of the characters is excellent. They all declaim in the same high falsetto voice, to an accompaniment of gongs and cymbals, but the mimicry and by-play are often cleverly done.

In a temple no one takes the slightest notice of any worshipper that may drop in except the priest who is engaged for the ceremony, and takes care to have forehand payment. When his devotions are over, a man sees no impropriety in taking the burning incense before his deity to light his pipe. There is no solemnity or reverence manifest, but a single syllable omitted, or a genuflection at the wrong place, necessitates the repetition of the whole ceremony. The priest would be quite ready to throw dice for double fees or quits with any one who desired his services.

Besides the three authorised religions there are numerous sects. The most important is the Mahometans, who form a considerable portion of the inhabitants in the north-west. They have been well-nigh exterminated in the south-west. All over China they are to be found in the towns, inn-keeping being their speciality. They are the loosest of all the professors of Islam, and are to be distinguished from other Chinese only by their aversion to pork and the absence of idols in their houses. They are not debarred from office, and many hold commissions in the army. As officers they have certain idolatrous rites to perform, but get over the difficulty by writing the characters *chen chu*, True Lord, their name for God, on a piece of red paper which is placed before the image or tablet. By this device the true believer saves his conscience and the latitudinarian Chinese are quite content with outward conformity. A bath sometimes in the mosque on Friday is the only religious duty required from the ordinary member. The mosque looks externally like an ordinary Chinese build-

ing. There are no minarets, and no public call
to prayer. Whether the latter is dispensed with
because it would be against the law, or because
it would not be responded to, is a matter of
doubt.

The other sects, like the White Lily sect, the
Vegetarians, the Religion of the Burning Lamp,
are treated as secret societies, and proscribed by
law. How far they are offshoots of Buddhism
and Taoism, and how far they are political in
their aims, it would be difficult to say. When a
mandarin excites a tumult by extortion, it is
always his safest cue to represent it as due to
a secret society which must be stamped out.
They have harped on the same string respecting
riots against Europeans, which have been proved
up to the hilt to be of their own instigation.

No one can tell what a Chinaman's religion is.
He observes all that I have described as primitive, with more or less mental reservation—the
worship of heaven and earth and of his ancestors.
He believes in luck, the *fung-shui*, ghosts, and
demons. He takes from Buddhism and Taoism

just what suits himself, and always contributes
to the temples of both sects. He attaches no
importance to such mummeries himself, but his
wife, his mother, or his neighbours are very
superstitious, and he is not a man to quarrel
about trifles. To oblige a friend he is quite
ready to add Christianity to his religious re-
pertory—but he does not believe in an exclusive
religion. He has been most aptly described
as an adherent of all sects and a member of
none. But he has no priest who is a minister
of all denominations, a phenomenon that sometimes makes an appearance to reply to a toast
at a public dinner. The civil magistrate is *ex
officio* the bishop of Confucianism. His magis-
tracy is his diocese, and the literati priests and
deacons. The priests of Budd and Tao must
be regularly ordained, or their ministrations are
good for nothing. Heresy does not mean the
holding of heterodox opinions, but unauthorised
additions or omissions in the ritual. A Chinaman is broad in his theology, high in his
ceremonial, and doubtful in his morality.

CHAPTER IV

GOVERNMENT AND MANDARINS. THE ARMY, LAW, AND MEDICINE

The Golden Age—Origin of the Chinese—Early Civilisation—
Power of Assimilation—The Emperor—Nobility—Officials—
The District Magistrate—His Duties—Administration of the
Law—Punishments—Aversion to Litigation—Self-made Men
—Pawnbrokers—A General Strike—The Army—Lawyers—
Doctors.

HAVING passed in review the notions which a
Chinaman is taught in the temple, at school, and
by the parental fireside, his political and civic
environment requires a brief notice before passing
on to his social and family life.

To understand other nationalities we must
know their history, but in the case of the Chinese
it is not necessary. There is nothing remarkable about Chinese history but its length and its
monotony. The Chinese youth is taught that
Panku hewed out the heavens and the earth—the
permutations of the *yang* and *ying* having appar-

ently left them in a very chaotic state. Then
came the emperors of Heaven, Earth, and Man,
who reigned respectively 30,000, 20,000, and
10,000 years. Suijen discovered fire by rubbing
sticks. Yenchow taught men to build huts of
branches. In B.C. 2852 came Fuh-hi who taught
hunting, fishing, pasturage; established marriage,
appointed magistrates, made musical instruments,
and taught writing which superseded the use of
knotted cords. He reigned 115 years. The next
emperor, Shen-nung taught agriculture and established markets. Then came Whang-ti, who made
pottery, wrought in metals, constructed a
calendar, discovered the medicinal properties of
plants, and divided China into provinces. His
queen reared silkworms and taught the arts of
spinning and weaving. Respectable Chinese
historians treat this period as mythical, but the
conviction is ingrained that civilization had its
origin in the Flowery Land.

In B.C. 2356 came the Confucian paragon, the
Emperor Yao. " He was reverential, intelligent,
accomplished, and thoughtful — naturally and

without effort." "He regulated and polished the
people. The result was universal concord." Yao
looked out a worthy successor in Shun, having
taken him from the "ditches" and married him
to his daughter to test his fitness to bear rule.
Yao's own son was unworthy, and he was set to
dig the ditches. According to Confucius, Shun
was "profound, wise, accomplished, intelligent,
mild, respectful, and entirely sincere." Shun's
son Yu drained the country which had been
inundated by the Yellow River. This was China's
golden age. A Chinaman's idea of progress is
backwards, to make things as nearly as possible
what he thinks they were 4000 years ago.

If this age ever existed, it has left no traces but
in the Confucian Classics. It was followed by a
long era of wars and intrigues among petty states,
which were joined in a loose confederacy. The
first ascertained date in Chinese history is an
eclipse of the sun, B.C. 775. Confucius could
trace the annals of his own native state of Lu
back only to B.C. 722. The Chinese people did
not have their origin then by any means, but it is

absurd to designate what goes before with the name of history.

China really appears to have been peopled by successive waves of emigrants, more skilful both in peace and war than the aborigines, who came from the North-West, down the basin of the Yellow River. They were an agricultural people, dwelling in walled villages, and pushed out fresh settlements among the ruder tribes, who lived by fishing and hunting. Confucius makes Yu to have ruled over an empire as extensive as modern China, but although born in Shantung himself, he never saw the sea, the whole sea-board then being occupied by "barbarians." There are still many remnants of these tribes in the mountains of the south and west. Some appear to be allied to the Thibetans, but most are kindred to the Burmese. They have been partly exterminated and still more largely absorbed by the Chinese, whose civilisation has far greater power of assimilating lower races than ours. Near Ichang there was a small native state which was only subjugated in the last century. Forty of the chiefs were entrapped and massacred. The rest of the tribesmen were merely compelled to adopt the Chinese dress and customs and obey Chinese magistrates. Already there is no vestige of the old language left, and nothing to remind the traveller that the people and district have not always been thoroughly Chinese.

Since Shih Whang-ti instituted the present order in B.C. 221, there have been many revolutions but no change. He built the great wall after he had driven back the Hiung-nu, or Huns, and ever since China has remained isolated and unchangeable, the Tartar races, who have entered as conquerors, becoming in a short time as Chinese as the Chinese themselves.

The emperor or Whang-ti—the term is almost equivalent to the Roman *Deus Augustus*—styles himself the Solitary Man or the Son of Heaven, claiming to be the divine vicegerent upon earth. He is above all kings and princes, and it is contrary to the traditions of Peking to treat with other nations upon equal terms. The proof of these pretensions is the fact that Heaven has called him to sit on the Dragon Throne ; but he must make good his authority by ruling well. The right of rebellion is part of the Chinese constitution. A successful rebel would at once be hailed as emperor by divine right. The emperor *de facto* is to every good Confucianist the emperor *de jure*.

The emperor's person is sacred and his attributes more than human. With a stroke of the vermilion pencil he promotes and degrades the gods as freely as his own officials. Meritorious mandarins are canonized at death and temples raised in their honour.

Nominally the emperor's will is supreme, but no constitutional monarch is so much bound by law as he is by custom. Night and day, sleeping and waking, two mandarins keep watch over him. Should his majesty's appetite be deficient, the court physicians are immediately called in to administer physic. They draw salary as long as he is well, but their pay ceases when he is sick. The emperor never leaves the palace grounds except to worship at the imperial graves. Then a number of close sedan chairs are provided, the same as that which he occupies; the people have to shut their doors and windows, and any one caught peeping at the cavalcade is instantly beheaded. He is a mere puppet in the hands of the palace eunuchs. The real power is divided between the Tartar princes and high Chinese officials.

Amongst the Chinese proper there is no nobility. There are many decorations like our orders of knighthood, and five ancient titles of nobility are also bestowed, but the rank descends a step with each generation and soon becomes extinct. They are mere titles of honour and carry with them no legislative or executive powers, and as a rule the emperor prefers to ennoble a man's deceased ancestors and not his unborn descendants. All honours conferred are also liable to be revoked by a stroke of the pencil.

There is no semblance of a parliament. The government is carried on by six administrative boards at Peking, and Viceroys, Governors and inferior mandarins in the provinces. Next to the Governor are the Provincial Treasurer, Provincial Judge, and Literary Chancellor; then come Intendants of Circuit, Prefects, and District Magistrates. This is the regular gradation, but there are many special appointments.

The District Magistrate is the mandarin *par excellence*. It is only with him that our typical Chinaman comes into contact; and the less the better, as when summoned to appear before him, he grimly remarks that he is going to hell. The district or *shien* corresponds to our counties, being of no fixed size. The eighteen provinces are divided into more than 1200 districts. The District Magistrate is styled the *Chi-shien*—the man who knows the *shien*. He is judge, jury, and counsel on both sides in all criminal and civil lawsuits; he is public prosecutor, head jailor, and chief of police; he takes the census and inspects education; he is collector of excise and customs, surveyor of public works and board of trade; he has charge of canals, roads, embankments, and bridges; he is held responsible for robbery, rebellion, and breaches of the moral law ; he has to keep the city walls in repair, inspect the militia, see that the officers do their duty, regulate the temples and the priesthood, and on many occasions act as high priest himself. The blame is fastened upon him for floods and droughts, and at such times he has to head processions of country people, clad in sackcloth and carrying three burning joss sticks in his hand. In drought he orders the South Gate of the city to be closed, and in excessive rain the North. He then proclaims a time of fasting and humiliation to last three days, during which no animal may be killed or any flesh exposed for sale.

To obtain office is the goal of every Chinaman's ambition. The road to preferment lies through the Literary Examinations, but it may also be obtained by special merit. For a long time this latter has been the most frequented path, and but one consideration has been accounted merit—a sufficient bribe. To assist in his duties, the mandarin has at his own expense to maintain a staff of secretaries and clerks and a whole regiment of underlings. His pay is ordinarily about one tenth of his necessary expenses, but as he is collector of local revenue and disburser of local expenses, something may be saved off the balance that should go to the provincial treasury, and there are other methods by which he is able to recoup himself during the three years for which he holds office. No one can be a magistrate in his native province.

Chinese law is codified, but the code is rarely appealed to, the principles laid down in the Confucian classics and local usage deciding the case. A point of equity would always overrule a point of law. Prisoners and witnesses are examined by the magistrate, who administers the bamboo freely to elicit the truth, and for the recalcitrant and evasive has more refined methods—suspension by the thumbs, stretching on the rack, the insertion of small pieces of bamboo below the nails, and kneeling on broken crockery and hot chains. No oath is ever administered, as none has been discovered that is binding on the Chinese conscience. The only way of avoiding these inconveniences, if one has the misfortune to be involved in the toils of the law, is the use of palm oil. The law is swift and sure and eminently satisfactory to the man who has a well-filled purse and will use it freely. No advocates are allowed, but I could never get a Chinaman to admit that it was a disadvantage—it is the surer method to fee the judge.

The punishments are barbarous. The prisons are filthy dens in which criminals and those under arrest herd together. A newcomer has to pay his first-footing to the older inmates on arrival. The rations are barely sufficient to sustain life, but any luxuries, or even a day out to visit one's friends, may be obtained by paying the jailor. Petty offences are punished by the bamboo, which is applied to the proper part, and not as the bastinado. Others are sent out with a wooden collar, the cangue, round their neck—a sort of portable pillory, bearing a label detailing their offences. Capital punishment is usually by beheading with a sword, sometimes by strangling; and very often in Ichang criminals are exposed

in wooden cages in the streets until they die of
thirst and hunger. In a neighbouring district
they are placed up to the waist in a barrel of
quick-lime. A magistrate at Ichang put a man
to death by suspending him at the top of a pole
by a hand and a foot. The case was reported
and he narrowly escaped degradation, not on
account of cruelty, but for introducing an innovation.

The principles of equity are the same everywhere, but Chinese law takes a peculiar view in
some cases. Embezzlement from an employer is
a lighter crime than ordinary theft. You ought
to employ only honest men, but you cannot
guard against a thief. For a servant who was
paid starvation wages to help himself, would not
be regarded as an offence at all. Forgery would
generally be treated as a case of ordinary fraud.

A Chinaman always tries to avoid going to
law, and has very little sympathy with those who
feel its lash. A good neighbour will settle his
disputes quietly by arbitration ; and criminals he
holds, if not guilty of one offence, have very likely

committed another. He has no admiration for self-made men, unless they have made themselves by their brains at the public examinations. He never boasts that he is self-made, for that would be to cast a slur on his worthy ancestors ; and he is never ashamed of his poor relations. When some one who has rapidly become rich is pounced upon by the harpies of the yamen, as the official residence and court-house are called—being both in the same building—he grins with inward satisfaction. The yamen runners have a keen scent for prey, and the risk of having a case trumped up against him, which will cost money to get clear of, is one to which the capitalist is constantly exposed.

Pawnbrokers are wealthy and important personages. A mandarin who was leaving Ichang thought he would have something out of one of them, and sent a company of yamen runners with a number of empty boxes to the pawnshop. They had a long list of pretended valuables, said to be inside, which they were commissioned to pawn for nearly £150. The pawnbroker demurred, and wished a sight of the pledges. On this the yamen runners threw down the boxes in his shop, and refused to remain with a man who doubted the magistrate's list or questioned the values he had affixed. The boxes were in due course sent for by the mandarin, opened, and found empty, on which the pawnbroker was arrested on a charge of theft. He had little profit off that year's business. A man who lived next door to me was glad to hush up for a thousand dollars a charge of treason, because some children had fired a cracker, a sign of rejoicing, in the courtyard of his house on a day set apart for mourning for the deceased Empress. A competent mandarin has many ways of eking out his salary. Self-made men are safe game, but he has to respect the old and well connected families of the district. The literati and gentry, as they are called, have a distinct standing, and meet together in council. They could defy any magistrate, but he has sufficient sympathy with the class he belongs to himself rarely to come in conflict with them.

It pays everybody to keep on terms with the mandarin, but some of them are rapacious beyond even Chinese endurance. In such a case there may be a riot, but the more characteristic way is to institute a general strike. The great man wakens some morning to find no barber in attendance to shave his head and trim his pigtail. His butler tells him the barbers are on strike. Presently the cook returns with an empty basket—there is nothing in the market, and the shops are shut. His excellency must breakfast off the broken victuals of yesterday. He calls his sedan chair—it is not the proper thing for a magistrate to walk on foot—to go out and see what is the matter. There are no chair-bearers; they have decided not to work to-day. By this time a crowd of coolies has collected in the courtyard of the yamen, beseeching the father and mother of the people to give them work or rice. If he try to disperse the mob by force, there will be blows upon both sides and blood will be spilt. Then messengers will be sent post haste to inform the Viceroy or Intendant of Circuit. A regiment of soldiers will be sent down to restore order, and an investigation will be held. One or two will lose their heads as being ringleaders in the disturbance, but the real instigators are quite safe—no evidence will be forthcoming but against some bad characters who are a pest to the town. In any case, the mandarin will be stripped of his decorations and dismissed the service for incapacity; if he be fortunate enough to avoid a graver charge. These disturbances are generally caused by some increase of the taxes or stricter methods of levying them. If wise, the mandarin requests a few of the head men to *sang liang*, discuss the situation, and makes the desired concessions. Order is restored at once, and the people quietly resume business. There is very little real public feeling, and individual cases of injustice and extortion, while they add nothing to a magistrate's popularity, rarely produce a tumult. But it is otherwise when the craft of a class is in danger.

The Chinaman does not like soldiers and soldiering. He has no ambition for bubble reputation at the cannon's mouth. "Good iron is not made into nails, nor are good men turned into soldiers." But the Chinaman is no coward, although the stigma is often fastened to him. He is a plain matter of fact man, and does not see the glory of making his body a target for a miserable shilling a day. When there are bullets flying he endeavours to get out of the way. When tired of his life he commits suicide; but faces danger like a man in the course of his calling when there is money to be made.

The Tartar Bannermen form a royal bodyguard, and garrison a few Chinese towns. They are soldiers by birth and profession, drawing an allowance from the day they are born, and buried at the expense of the exchequer. Except the large feet of their women, there is little to distinguish them from ordinary Chinese, with whom they are not allowed to intermarry.

The army proper consists of provincial fencibles, a certain number being maintained in each prefecture from local revenue. Their chief duties are to put down brigandage, guard the cities, and escort the civil mandarins. Every soldier carries a fan and an umbrella. They are armed anyhow, with bamboo spears, bows and arrows, native matchlocks, or discarded European muskets. The colonel rides a mule or a pony, which his attendant generally holds by the tail. When his regiment goes through drill, he sits in a folding chair and regales himself with a cup of tea. Military tactics are designed to frighten more than to fight an enemy. The display of flags and banners is terrible, and attached to each battalion is a troop of boys dressed in yellow skin-tights with black stripes to resemble tigers. Others carry bamboo shields with a devil's head painted on them to inspire terror.

The pay of a soldier is fairly good for China, about £1 a month—when he gets it. If the pay be irregular, his discipline is lax. He is permitted to take his gun and shoot game in the hills at any time. Others turn their uniform inside out and work as ordinary labourers, except when required for a review, or ordered to turn out on the arrival or departure of a mandarin. Their numbers are far beneath the regulation strength. The Ichang prefecture had an establishment of 3000, and deducted pay for as many from the local revenue. About 300 soldiers were actually kept, the balance of pay finding its way into the pockets of the civil and military authorities. This alone must have represented a squeeze of £30,000 a year, and it was not the best egg in the mandarin basket.

When the provincial authorities came on a tour of inspection the whole city was paralysed. Every labourer in town seemed to have turned soldier. Dilapidated uniforms and rusty weapons were turned out. Three thousand men of some kind were presented on the parade ground, and the inspecting officer drew up his report in strict accordance with the "refresher" received.

For foreign wars volunteers are enrolled. These are the Chinese "braves," so called from the character *yung*, brave, being very conspicuously painted on their jackets. When a district is called upon to furnish so many volunteers, the mandarin first clears out the prison and enrolls the sweepings of the opium dens, then presses all "known to the police" who can carry a rifle, and sends off the rag-tag of the district as food for powder. The wonder is that they fight so well as they do. At Tientsin Li Hung-Chang had about 60,000 troops drilled and armed on a European model. Some of the other Viceroys have a few thousand troops worth the name, but the rank and file of the Chinese army is of the character described. Only those who judged the Chinese forces from these picked specimens could have been surprised at the result of the war with Japan.

If the average Chinaman has no love for the civil powers he likes the military still less. I remarked to an old disciple of Confucius who was telling me how Pao-chow had risen from selling fruit in the streets of Ichang to be a great Chinese general, that he must be a man

of remarkable ability. "Ability: what kind of
ability is required to commit murder?"

Having dealt with the other liberal profes-
sions, we may finish law and pass on to medicine.
Although no advocates may appear in court, a
number of broken down schoolmasters pick up
a precarious living by writing out petitions for
litigants. A civil suit must originate in a petition
to the mandarin. To get it presented, the door-
keeper of the yamen must first be feed, and
every secretary through whose hands it passes
must receive an honorarium. When it reaches
the great man, a suitable tribute must be paid
to his justice; and the man who wishes to gain
his case will take care to enlist the sympathies
of the mandarin's lackey and his wife's nurse.
The pettifogger alluded to will provide witnesses
well drilled in the evidence they are to give.
In China the law has risks both for the counsel
and his client. It is a statutory offence to aid
and abet in lawsuits. A Chinese lawyer has to
reckon upon the chances of the bamboo, just as

a French editor counts upon the probabilities of
a duel.

The faculty of medicine is almost at as low
an ebb as the church and the bar. There are
no medical schools, and any one may practise
as a doctor who can find patients. The only
approach to a diploma is to give out that one's
ancestors have professed the healing art for three
or seven generations. Dissection is not practised
and would not be permitted. They have the
crudest notions of anatomy and the functions of
the various organs. Their treatment of disease
is allopathic; and the ills that flesh is heir to
are divided into four classes, hot and cold, dry
and wet, which are to be combated by appropriate antidotes. They believe in adjuvants,
and no physic will be effective without the proper
yin-si. They diagnose almost entirely by feeling
the pulse. This is done by placing three fingers
on the wrist, one for the pulse of the heart,
another for that of the lungs, and the third for
the pulse of the liver. A skilful doctor will feel
the pulse of a lady of quality, who cannot be

seen by male visitors, by sitting in an adjoining room and holding the end of a silken cord which is tied round her wrist. Most patients bargain with the doctor; so much for a cure, and nothing if he fails. A town physician in good practice will not descend to this, but rides in a sedan chair and charges as much as a shilling a visit. He writes his prescriptions, which are dispensed at the drug shop. The ordinary practitioner keeps his own drugs, and never turns away a patient.

For those who can afford it Corean ginseng, worth almost its weight in gold, is a specific for all diseases. The pharmacopœia contains rhubarb, gentian, catechu, cardamums, nux vomica, camphor, liquorice, sulphate of iron, nitre, preparations of arsenic and mercury, and many other drugs used in Europe. But it contains a far greater number of such substances as tiger's bones, serpent's skins and serpent's dung, which is used as an eye salve, dried centipedes, toad's skin; every plant that grows and some part of every animal that breathes. A prescription usually contains twenty or thirty ingredients; and although they have many valuable drugs, they cannot be acquainted with their individual properties. For ordinary diseases they have doubtless discovered homely cures, but no doctor ever refuses to treat a case, whether he knows anything about it or not. Having no knowledge of anatomy or physiology, their identification of diseases must be most unreliable. They have no tinctures or extracts or medical preparations. The patient buys the raw materials and infuses them, and drinks off the decoction at a draught. The remains of the prescription left in the pot are thrown into the street, under the charitable impression that the unwary traveller who treads upon the mess will carry off the patient's disease. Though they make no tinctures or extracts, they are fond of pills and boluses and plasters. A Chinaman is always taking medicine. When ill he takes it as a cure, and when well as a preventative of sickness.

In medicine they are probably not above two centuries behind Europe, but their surgery is worse than nothing.   Their one operation is acupuncture.   Into any swelling or tumour in any part of the body they are ready to thrust a needle to let out the wind. A man suffering from dropsy declares that it is wind, and the doctor treats him by prescribing antidotes for that element.   On no account will they suffer an open sore.   As soon as an abscess bursts, the surgeon sticks on a black plaster to keep in the pus.   If allowed to escape, the substance and vitality of his body would ooze out.   When the matter burrows and makes a fresh exit by the side of the plaster, another is put over the new opening. This will go on till the whole mass, plasters and all, falls away, leaving a huge ulcer.   There are tens of thousands of Chinese maimed for life by the mistreatment of a simple boil.   As in other warm countries, inflammation of the eyes is common, but the medical faculty is chiefly responsible for the extraordinary number of the blind.

The Chinese have a horror of amputation, which they look upon as a mutilation of the body,

and fear to be sent halt and lame into the other
world. A patient in a mission hospital often
prefers death to the loss of a hand or foot. For
this reason exposure in the cage is considered a
more merciful punishment than decapitation, and
the relatives of a man who has been beheaded
petition the magistrate for leave to sew his head
on again, a favour that is seldom granted, the head
being exposed over the city gate.

Bone setting is a separate art. They use no
splints, but bind up the broken limb with the
pliant bark of the *kow* tree. This speedily hardens,
and the results are frequently satisfactory. Tooth-
ache is ascribed to the presence of a worm, the
extraction of which is undertaken by old women,
who never fail to produce the maggot, after
poking in the sufferer's mouth with a rusty wire.
Wounds are dressed with the universal black
plaster, a poultice of cow dung, or the half burnt
skin of a dog. The least objectionable method
is to bring the edges together and cover the part
with the fresh skin of a fowl which adheres
firmly.

Many of their cures are highly fanciful. For baldness they prescribe soup made with a hedgehog. For paralysis they infuse the claws of owls and kites. For jaundice they administer a handful of wood lice; *Scottice*, sclaters. Wine in which tiger's bones have been steeped is very strengthening; so are the lights of a pig, which are the dearest flesh in the market. For consumption and general debility they prescribe human milk. It is extremely valuable in old age; and as it is not proper for a young woman to approach any man but her husband, a hole is made in the partition between two rooms through which the wet nurse thrusts her breast and the old gentleman sucks from the other side.

Doctors are the principal people who advertise, posting imposing bills setting forth their nostrums. Their cures are secret traditions in the family, and the doctor is careful to gather his herbs in the right quarter of the moon and under a favourable conjunction of the planets. When a man is sick he is just as likely to call in a Taoist priest to charm away the demon that causes the disease as to seek aid from the doctor. Either plan is likely to be efficacious, for, as evidenced by the mission hospitals, the Chinaman is endowed with remarkable recuperative powers.

CHAPTER V

LAND AND TAXES

Land Tenure—Minerals—Mining—Coal—Salt—Transfer of Land
—Tenants—Agriculture—Native Opium—Manuring—Pisciculture — Market Gardening — Custom Houses — Cause of
Riots—I. M. Customs—Direct Taxation—Canals—Embankments—Irrigation—The Great Wall—City Walls—Roads.

THE land of China all belongs to the Emperor
as ultimate proprietor, and is subject to a small
land tax, which varies according to soil and
situation. This tax is payable at an office
attached to the yamen of the district magistrate, and, before the development of foreign
trade and the establishment of the Maritime
Customs, was the most important source of imperial revenue. A list is kept of all the land
in the district and its possessors. Non-payment
of the tax for three years may lead to for-
feiture, and the law does not undertake to pro-
tect the interests of absentees. To have paid
the land tax on any property for three successive

years without challenge, is a valid title to ownership.

The possessor has a perpetual right of occu-
pancy, which he may transfer, sell, or mortgage,
and he may use the land as he pleases for
agricultural and building purposes. He may
open quarries and clay pits, but he has no
claim to the minerals in the bowels of the
earth. There is little difficulty about extract-
ing coal and iron in the native fashion at the
outcrop of the beds, but for the opening of
regular mines an imperial license would be
required, and a royalty would be charged. The
government is very chary in granting such
privileges, and all attempts made hitherto to
mine in the European manner have been
carried on by the government, or under direct
government control. Even could a permit be
obtained, no Chinese would put their money
in such a venture, knowing that under some
pretext or other the mandarins would appropriate the profit, if there was any. The
country has not been surveyed, but has been

traversed by competent geologists, and is known to be extremely rich in minerals. Coal is to be had plentifully and cheap in most districts, and iron is abundant. The steamers running to Ichang mostly used the native coal. The chief difficulty was to procure a steady supply of uniform quality. The best was of good steaming quality, and for household purposes no better need be desired ; but although produced in the district the transport was so dear that it could not be delivered much under a pound a ton. Copper, lead, white copper (a native alloy of various metals), silver, gold, nitre, sulphur, salt, gypsum, etc., are produced by native processes. The minerals will at some period be an inexhaustible source of revenue and national wealth. At present there is little got from anything but salt.

Salt is a government monopoly, and none is allowed to be imported from abroad. It is wrought in the provinces of Ngan-whui and Sz-chuan, both in the form of rock salt and brine. The brine is got from artesian wells,

which the Chinese have known how to bore
for ages. In Sz-chuan the brine is evaporated
by an inflammable gas which escapes from
fissures in the earth, and is conducted in bamboo pipes to the salt works. The salt is
heavily taxed at the mine, and in the course
of transport through the empire is subjected
to frequent duties both for local and imperial
revenue. The retail price at Ichang is about
two pence halfpenny a pound.

The transfer of land is extremely simple.
When the price is agreed upon, a deed is
written out in plain terms stating the boundaries and size of the property, the names of
the adjacent owners, and the price stipulated.
To this document, which any man of ordinary
education is competent to draw up, several
local witnesses affix their signature. It is then
taken to the district magistrate, who notifies
the neighbouring proprietors to see that the
boundaries are correct, and if there be no complaint lodged, he affixes his seal, charging a

certain commission on the price. It usually amounts to three per cent, but the cautious investor waits until the mandarin's triennial term of office is on the point of expiry, when he can be got to transact business on more reasonable terms rather than leave the ingathering of the fees to his successor. The new proprietor's name is enrolled for the payment of the land tax, and there is no further formality. Disputes about ownership are rare.

When a person lets his land the law is very favourable to the tenant. Money rents are unknown. The landlord bargains for a fixed portion of the chief crops, which is estimated at so many tenths. The winter crops and minor products usually belong entirely to the tenant. When the harvest is reaped, the landlord may claim his share, or the amount is settled by mutual valuation. No lease is necessary. So long as a tenant cultivates the land, he cannot be evicted, nor can the rent tithes be increased on him. If he farms well, it is for the advantage of both parties; and the landlord and tenant have an equal interest in effecting permanent improvements and keeping the soil in good heart. Buildings give little trouble; mud, bamboo, and thatch are plentiful, and the farmer repairs his steading in his spare time. Sons and other direct heirs may claim the tenancy on the old terms, but there is no right of sale. A tenant may leave at any time, but he must leave all improvements to the landlord without compensation. This apparent injustice is an intentional device to get the people rooted to their paternal acres, upon which all Confucian economists declare the stability of the empire to depend. There are few large estates, and such as exist, are in a multitude of detached patches. In the Ichang district one half of the farmers own their own land. I have known good rice land sold for £80 an acre. The Chinese farmer leads a frugal and laborious life. He seldom makes much money, but he has always an abundance of the necessaries of life, and unlike the Indian ryot is not under the thumb of the money lender. That harpy, who battens under the clemency of British rule, would not thrive under the patriarchal government of the mandarins. These gentry may oppress the people themselves, but they deserve all credit for permitting no one else to do so. A fat usurer would be a rare caption for the myrmidons of the yamen. A kind providence has so ordered that one evil is usually destructive of another.

In outlying parts of the empire there are tracts of unoccupied land, given in allotments to emigrants who will settle and cultivate them, paying land tax after a term of years. In settled districts the uncultivated land is all in the hands of private owners, but as an incentive to reclamation no tax is levied upon new land for a considerable period. There is a right of way everywhere except through growing crops, but indiscriminate pasturage and cutting of trees and herbage are not permitted. The tracts covered with graves in the vicinity of towns are treated as public pasturages, but any injury done to the graves is severely punished. There are no game laws; and all the Justices in the

United Kingdom would fail to convince John Chinaman that any one could have property in wild animals until he had succeeded in catching them.

Milk is not used as an article of diet, and butter and cheese are unknown. Goat flesh is eaten in winter, but considered too heating in summer. Sheep—only the fat-tailed variety is known—do not thrive in the Ichang district. The common ox and the water buffalo are both used in ploughing. Their flesh is little esteemed, and is the cheapest in the market; but as they are not fattened for the butcher, the only beef to be obtained is from animals that are past work, or have died of disease. There is in Ichang a law, enforced by the bamboo, against slaughtering healthy cattle. They should be employed in the labours of the field, and their destruction is regarded as killing the goose that lays the golden eggs. Pork and poultry are the favourite articles of flesh diet, and agriculture has to adapt itself to the tastes of consumers. There are no large horses, but

ponies, mules, and donkeys are used for riding
and carrying burdens.

Sufficient pasturage for all requirements is
found on the hills, among the graves, and on
the banks of canals and streams. Agricultural
land is never sown out in grass, but the Chinese
are very careful to attend to the rotation of
crops. In a country of such vast extent and
variety of climate there are many local differ-
ences, but the methods employed at Ichang
hold generally true for the greater part of
China. Tillage is effected partly by a primitive
plough, little better than a crooked stick shod
with iron, drawn by an ox or buffalo, and partly
by digging, not with a spade, but with a powerful mattock or pick-axe. The fields are small,
often no larger than garden plots, and they are
as carefully hoed and kept as free of weeds.
The farms seldom exceed twenty acres. When
water can be had for rice cultivation, the fields
are levelled, in terraces if need be, and channels
made for irrigation, the same as in sewage farms
at home. Where even Chinese ingenuity and

Chinese labour cannot procure an adequate supply of water, the land is allowed to retain its natural configuration. There are few fences. Rice is thickly sown in seed plots, which are completely covered with water. The rice fields are prepared by digging and ploughing; then the water is turned on, and the farmer continues his work with a heavy harrow drawn by an ox, until not a clod is left, himself wading over the knees in mud. When the seedling rice attains the height of four or six inches, it is planted out in the fields of liquid mud. The tufts speedily take root, and the fields are kept covered with water until the grain begins to ripen, when it is run off. The rice is reaped by sickle, and after a short exposure to the strong sun is beaten out by the flail, or trodden out by (muzzled) oxen on a threshing floor composed of hard earth. If the season be early, there is sometimes a second crop of rice, which pays best of all field produce.

The chief summer crops grown on dry land are cotton, Indian corn, sesamum, and tall millet,

with small millet, sweet potatoes, and ground
nuts upon poor sandy soil. Buckwheat is also
a principal summer crop on poor land, and, along
with radishes, it is a favourite autumn crop. Our
ordinary cereals are winter crops, sown in Nov-
ember and reaped in April. Wheat, barley, peas,
and beans are extensively grown. A farmer has
always two crops off the same ground in the
course of a year, and sometimes three ; but occasionally it is thought more profitable to work a
rice field as fallow in winter than to crop it. I
never saw rye in China ; and oats, a wretched
bearded variety, are only grown on the tops of
high hills. Below oats comes the common potato,
then millet and Indian corn. To live upon oats
and potatoes is the Chinese picture of misery,
and the person who has only such fare as wheat,
millet, and Indian corn is said to "eat bitterness,"
and is considered to have neither the strength
nor the ability of his compatriot who sits down
to three or four great bowlfuls of boiled rice twice
a day. Contrary to the Irish opinion, there is a
strong prejudice against the potato as being ad-

verse to fecundity. Great quantities of rape are
grown in winter for oil from the seed, which is
used in cooking. Tall millet is chiefly employed
for the distillation of *samshu*, a sort of coarse
whisky. Sesamum and ground nuts supply a
superior culinary oil. Beans and peas are made
into *towfu*, a white cheesy-looking substance of
the consistence of curds. It is eaten along with
boiled rice, and the Chinese are fond of it, but
few Europeans succeed in acquiring the taste.
The peas and beans are ground up wet and
steeped in vats, the whole process resembling
the old Scotch method of preparing sowens.
Indian corn is made into vermicelli and "corn-
flour." Wheat and barley flour is made into a
great variety of scones and cakes, some sweet,
some seasoned with salt and garlic, and many
cooked in boiling oil. It is also baked into a
sort of steamed bread, but rice is the Chinaman's
staff of life.

Opium is extensively grown in the Ichang
prefecture, and that produced in the district of
Patung is now said to compare favourably with

the best that comes from India, greater care having been bestowed upon it since the semblance of prohibition was removed. It is a profitable crop, but exhausts the soil. The native product is about half the price of the Indian drug, and will certainly drive it from the Chinese market in a few years. There are no reliable statistics, but it is well within the mark to say that China already produces three-fourths of the quantity she consumes. Opium was known and grown in China before the East India Company sent an ounce to Canton.

Most farmers have a few mulberry trees about their houses and the boundaries of their fields. The silk industry is capable of indefinite expansion, and little is needed but greater care in winding to command a still higher price in the foreign market. The cocoon ends, which used to be thrown away by the natives, are now sold to foreign merchants, who export them to Europe to be worked up by improved machinery. Tea is grown in many parts of the country, but in strictly circumscribed areas. I have seen it cultivated on one side of a ravine and not at all upon the other when there was a change in the geological formation. It is a grocers' puff to speak of the tea gardens of China. Each farmer has a few bushes, and when intended for foreign export he sells the green leaves to the country general merchant. The different varieties of China tea are produced by the skill of the native middlemen in sorting and curing. The Chinese themselves give by far the best price for leaf of a fine quality. The Russian merchants can afford to buy finer " chops " than could be profitably sold in London. The rubbish that the British matron insists upon having at eighteenpence a pound has in many cases already passed through a native teapot, and has been skilfully doctored by some Chinaman who has fired, rolled, and recoloured the leaf, and has again been further improved by the home mixer, who has added a quantity of strong Indian tea rich in tannin. The flavour of a really good tea is utterly destroyed by milk and sugar, which are accompaniments never used by the Chinese. They only sun-dry the leaf, and infuse it by pouring boiling water on a pinch in the bottom of the cup, nothing but inferior sorts being put in a teapot.

The live stock which a farmer rears for market consists of pigs and poultry, and possibly our depressed agriculturists might do worse than turn their attention more largely to these branches. Pork is worth from fourpence to fivepence a pound. A fowl sells from a shilling to eighteenpence, and eggs bring a farthing each, but they are mostly of small size.

The Chinese farmer pays great attention to manuring, and is incessant with the hoe. Every leaf and scrap, down even to the shavings of celestial scalps, carefully collected by the barber, find their way to the dung pit, and there are no wasted liquids about a homestead. The Chinaman eschews chemical manures, going upon the sensible theory of returning to the soil everything that comes from it. Night-soil is considered the best of all fertilizers, and every morning he goes before breakfast, when he commences the serious labours of the day,

with a pair of buckets to collect it in the towns
and villages. The method is as repulsive as it
is primitive, but if our farmers could devise
some practical way of utilizing sewage, they
would save their manure bills and increase
their crops; the rivers would not be polluted
nor would the citizens be poisoned with sewer
gas. In this matter and in land tenure, there
is reason to take a leaf out of the Chinaman's
book, with as satisfactory results as in the in-
stitution of competitive examinations for government employment, in which case we were not
ashamed to take the yellow man as our philosopher and guide.

The Chinaman knows how to cultivate the
water as well as the land. He rears oysters
extensively, and even contrives to stimulate the
bivalve to produce pearls. The Yangtse affords
an inexhaustible supply of some twenty varieties
of fish, and its waters are constantly swept by
every description of net and line. Cormorants
are trained to catch fish, and at Ichang, when

the net is put down, a tame otter is sent to raise the fish from the bottom, in much the same way as sportsmen employ a dog to find the game. At the proper season myriads of young sile are caught by gauze nets in the quiet nooks, and immediately transferred to a large earthenware jar. When this is full of tiny fish, about an inch in length, it is put in a creel, which the vendor carries on his back into districts removed from large streams. He sells the contents by the cupful to farmers to put in their ponds and reservoirs. Each cupful taken out, which has the appearance of thick broth, he replaces with a cupful of water, giving the fish room to grow as he peddles his ware. One wonders if the Fishery Board, with science and high salaries, has done as much to increase the food supply of the country as these humble Chinamen who pursue pisciculture for an honest penny.

The keeping of ducks is another characteristic Chinese industry. The duck feeder of the Yangtse has 600 to 1000 in his flock. He

rows a small boat in which he sleeps at night,
under a mat covering like a gipsy's tent, whilst
his flock is folded on the shore like sheep in a
stake net.   He moves up and down the river,
along the creeks and through the marshes with
his herd, resting in some convenient spot in
the breeding season.   The eggs find a ready
market at better prices than fowl's eggs, being,
when cured, a favourite delicacy, and no festive
board would be complete without salted duck.

As market gardeners the Chinese are un-
approachable.   I think all our vegetables, and
many more, are cultivated, except parsnips,
Swedish turnips, and beetroot.   Large radishes
generally take the place of the true turnip.   In
summer there is an endless variety of melons,
gourds,   cucumbers,   egg-plant,   chillies,   etc.
Garlic is very much used, and many varieties
of haricot beans.   The fruits at Ichang are
cherries, loquats, plums, apricots, peaches, pears
(large and coarse), apples (small crab), per-
simmons, oranges (common and Tangerine),
lemons, chesnuts, and walnuts.   To these may

be added the tallow, oil, and varnish trees, all important industries. In ponds and marshes the sacred lotus is much cultivated for the root, which is eaten as a vegetable, and made into arrow-root. The seeds are a delicacy. Marshes also supply the taro, the water-chesnut, and the water-caltrop. Indigo, hemp, linen from a species of nettle, and many other products are profitably produced in the district, but the account is not intended to be exhaustive, but merely to show the reader that the Chinaman knows how to take advantage of the resources of his country.

As already indicated, imperial revenue is largely dependent on the land and salt tax. Local revenue is derived from local custom-houses. These are exceedingly numerous, rendering it impossible to take anything to market without being pounced upon by the man at the receipt of custom. The roads leading to a city both by land and water are well guarded, and the squabbles are endless. The statutory rate is of little conse-

quence, as the men in charge have weights and
measures of their own, which they insist on using.
They would be afraid to write a receipt for a
wrong rate, but as to malpractices in the measuring, once the goods left their hands, they would
unblushingly aver that the aggrieved party had
not submitted the whole quantity to the court of
appeal. These devices are generally adverse to
the public, but when there is a choice of routes,
two custom-houses may compete for patronage.
As a means of counteracting smuggling and dis-
couraging the resort to a longer but less heavily
taxed road, native opium in transit through
Ichang used to be nominally taxed the proper
rate, but it was well known to the trade that
thirty two ounces were contained in the pound
weight that was used. For a short time, a Chinaman was in command of one of the river steamers,
and she mysteriously anchored about nightfall a
few miles below the city. The native captain
and the local officials were in some large smuggling concern to defraud the Maritime Customs,
and had their scouts watching the movements

of the European officers, rendering a seizure impossible. Tonnage dues are charged on junks navigating the rivers, as well as duty on their cargoes. Instead of being centralised, the native customs are sub-divided as much as possible among a multitude of "squeezing" stations. A big mandarin can always find employment for his poor relations in the native customs. Besides all these local custom houses for raising local revenue, there are *likin* barriers on all the great trade routes to collect money for imperial defence. A more rotten, inefficient, and irritating fiscal system it would be impossible to devise, and the only consideration that induces the Chinaman to submit to it is, when venality is so rife, the hope of getting his goods through cheaper than his rival. Produce and merchandise of every description in transit from one part of China to another have to pay toll to the authorities of each district they pass through. A basket of eggs is taxed before it can reach the market ; but I can remember the citizens of Aberdeen submitting to the same thing. The extension of steam navigation is opposed by the officials tooth and nail: no wonder! they can stop a junk and take their pound of flesh whenever they please, but goods sent by steamer pay two and a half per cent. transit duty and go past their squeezing barriers free. The introduction of railways would hit the mandarin pocket still more heavily, for the railway train like the steamboat would pay no toll by the way. There would be another universal two and a half per cent., which would frank goods to their destination. This in itself would be bad enough, but the last straw has been added by collecting this transit duty under European supervision and remitting it honestly to Peking. These considerations have ten times more weight than all other causes put together in repressing railways and obstructing steamers. The average Chinaman has no antipathy to either, but the mandarinate has raised the good old cry of Demetrius, "our craft is in danger," and *fung-shui* is the stalking-horse. This is the fanaticism at the root of all the riots in China; and if missions be struck at first, it is because they are regarded as the thin edge of the wedge.

The Maritime Customs have charge of foreign trade and coast and internal commerce, in so far as the transport is effected by steamers and sailing vessels of foreign build. On the Upper Yangtse, between Ichang and Chungking, foreign vessels are not allowed to run, but chartered junks may enter at the Maritime Customs and come under their regulations. A few articles are exempt from duty, and some others, notably tea and opium, pay higher rates, but the ordinary transit duty from the port of lading to the port of discharge, is two and a half per cent. *ad valorem*. In addition to this, there is a duty on all imports and exports of five per cent. Before reaching the consumer in the interior of China, foreign goods pay this seven and a half per cent., besides an indefinite amount of squeezes after leaving the river steamer. The Maritime Customs are under Sir Robert Hart, as Inspector General. There is an outdoor and indoor European staff composed of all nationalities, besides a large native staff of clerks, boatmen and messengers. There is an efficient medical service, accurate meteorological observations are taken, lighthouses, buoys, and all facilities for navigation maintained. All in all there is no better public service maintained by any country. The revenue is remitted directly to Peking, and is the only Chinese security the foreign money-lender will look at.

Individually small, for the most part, the multifarious and repeated duties levied on the Chinese are enormous in the aggregate; but they are mostly submitted to with passive resignation, the trader adding the amount to the price, and the consumer consoling himself with the reflection that he need not purchase if he dislikes the cost. There is no direct taxation, which would be most offensive to the Chinaman, who regards his house as his castle and his business as his own affair. He would keenly resent having the officials pry into the profits of the one, or appraise the value of the other; and to extract money for no service rendered or favour promised and without any hope of being recouped by the transaction, he would resist as violently as highway robbery. Far rather would the typical Chinaman put up with the mandarin's squeezes than submit to an income tax. Even when the mandarin sends a private messenger to inform the substantial merchant that official expenses are heavy and donations from patriotic citizens desirable, he grins and bears it, knowing that his voluntary gift will make a friend of the bench, should he be annoyed by a litigious customer. But ask questions about his income—you might as well send a sanitary inspector to his house; life would not be worth living upon these terms. Quite recently, there was an exodus from Hongkong when the latter was attempted.

The public works of greatest importance are the canals and river embankments. The Grand Canal from Peking to Hangchow is over 600 miles in length. It was made by Kublai Khan, who was emperor of China from 1260 to 1295

A.D. From Cambula, or Peking, he ruled from the Baltic to the Yellow Sea, from the Himalayas to the Frozen Ocean. He has probably a better title to Universal Conqueror than any other monarch, and none has perpetuated his memory and enlightened rule by a grander monument. There are numerous canals of lesser magnitude in many parts of China, which joined to the excellent natural waterways provide large portions of the empire with better means of communication and transport than were possessed by our own country before the introduction of railways.

Immense tracts of fertile and densely populated land have been rescued from the water. From the earliest ages to the present day, the Yellow river has been "China's Sorrow." The Chinese are no despicable hydraulic engineers. When the Yellow River last burst its banks and spread devastation far and wide, Dutch experts pronounced the stoppage of the breach almost impossible. Yet the Chinese effected it by native methods. On the Yangtse, whose rise in summer by the spring rains and melting of the snow in Thibet is from 35 to 45 feet, there are miles on miles of huge embankments, sometimes faced with hewn stones. Were the dykes to give way when the river is in flood, the town of Shasi, with• 200,000 inhabitants would be engulphed in 30 feet of water. One may travel in summer day after day on the plain of Hupeh and see the boats many feet above his head.

Irrigation is fully as important as drainage. A stream is not left to babble idly down a hillside, but is twisted and turned and drained off in a hundred rills to irrigate the face of the mountain which is cut into terraces, and what would naturally be an arid barren moor is converted into fertile rice fields. Rain water is stored in huge reservoirs, and not unfrequently a mountain glen is blocked by an embankment and made a gigantic tank. When gravitation will not serve, they use a variety of ingenious machines for raising water to irrigate the fields. But all these undertakings are carried through by private enterprise, whilst canals and embankments are in charge of the authorities.

K

Another remarkable public work is the Great Wall, which was built by Shih Whang-ti 200 years before Christ. It is from 15 to 30 feet high, with sufficient space on the top for the defenders, with a parapet for shelter, and towers at intervals, and is carried over hill and dale for 1250 miles. It was built to keep back the Tartars, but has never been effective in stopping an invasion; yet from the way it is spoken of by Chinese, it must have done good service in checking the roving hordes that were ready to sweep down upon every harvest. In every district there is a city, in which the *Chi-shien*, or District Magistrate, has his yamen. The cities are all walled in ancient fashion, and some are of great extent. The walls of Nanking are sixty miles in circuit, and it is a hard day's journey to walk round the walls of Wuchang, the provincial capital of Hupeh. The Ichang walls are two miles in circuit, and it is counted a small city. There are often tracts of gardens, parade grounds, and other open spaces within the walls, and the suburbs are frequently more busy and populous than the city proper. However large, towns without walls and a resident magistrate of the rank of *Chi-shien* are technically villages. To this category belongs Hankow, the great mart of central China, with a population of half a million at least. Wuchang, Hanyang, and Hankow practically form one town, separated only by the Yangtse and its tributary the Han, and must between them contain over a million people. City walls are from 20 feet to 30 feet high, 15 feet or more broad on the top, with a serrated and loop-holed parapet for defence, and arched gateways defended by a tower and platform for cannon. The walls are composed of an outer and inner casing of dressed stone, with the centre of beaten earth, the excavation of which forms the moat. To keep the city walls in repair is one of the prime duties of the magistrate. They would be no defence against a foreign enemy, but provide a sufficient refuge in cases of local rebellion, which are of more frequent occurrence than the outer world has any knowledge of. In remote country places

the peasants construct walled enclosures on the
top of isolated hills, to which they can retire in
danger.

Roads and bridges are also under the care of
the magistrates, but China is still waiting for her
General Wade. Inland transport in the northern
provinces is mainly by mule-cart, but the roads
have generally received no making but what has
been given by the traffic of ages. They are
alternately channels of dust and ditches of mud.
Macadamising is unknown, and where the roads
have been made, they are paved with great
stones, and being kept in no repair, these are
tilted at all angles. Their last state is worse
than their first. In Central China the roads are
mere foot paths. The imperial post road from
Peking to the South-West provinces and frontier
of Burmah passes through Ichang. It is about
six feet in breadth, a very poor proportion to its
length, and bears evidence of once being paved
in the centre. There are in the district a few
stone bridges of excellent construction, quite
equal to the very best that can be built in this

country. Over the smaller streams they place single slabs, sometimes 40 feet in length. These huge blocks are carried overland by lashing two strong beams to their sides, then making a net-work of smaller cross-beams and bamboos. A crowd of coolies get below the framework and walk off with it on their shoulders, like a nest of ants. The Chinese transported 80-ton guns in this manner, and sent boilers and machinery for woollen mills to the extreme north-west, which are now rusting on the steppes of Tartary. They also carried steam engines and mining plant to Yunnan, to the same bootless purpose. When they do appoint competent European managers, mandarin interference and corruption prevent the success of the enterprises. Railways would be comparatively useless without road-making, but progress in any direction is im-possible so long as industry and government are supposed to exist solely for the glory and emolu-ment of the men who either purchase office or get into power by their ability to write essays on Confucianism.

CHAPTER VI

SOCIAL LIFE

Headmen—·No Lapsed Masses—Trade Unions—Guilds—Strikes
—Literati and Gentry—Farmers—Artisans—Wages—Traders
—Bankers—Bargains—Transport—Inns—The Peace Kept—
The Chinaman on the British Constitution.

IT is not easy to say where government ends and
social life begins. Headmen play an important
part in public affairs, yet they hold no commission or official rank. Towns are divided into
wards, and country districts into *pu*, or parishes,
each having a headman and a constable, who are
appointed by the people, with the concurrence of
the magistrate. Last of all, a tything man is set
over every ten families, both in town and country.
He is supposed to know the members of each
household and their mode of living. These headmen adjust quarrels, and bring local wants before
the mandarin. They do much to promote the
peace and prosperity of the country, and it is
impossible not to be struck with the similarity of

150

the system to the organisation of the Jews and the original intention of the Presbyterian ruling eldership.

Rich and poor live together, and there is more familiarity between different classes than among ourselves. A labourer never appeals in vain to the man whom his mother or aunt has nursed. Then, a Chinaman has always his guild to fall back upon; and family feeling is very strong. They popularly speak of the "hundred names," but there are more Chinese surnames than that, although the number is not large. The people of the same name form in each district a sort of clan, with an ancestral temple of their own. They are ready, often too ready, to espouse the cause of a clansman. From the causes enumerated and other influences working in the same direction, it comes to pass that no Chinaman is isolated, or prevented by mere poverty from having some person of influence to go to in his difficulties, who will advise him kindly and give him a helping hand. Overcrowded as she is, with multitudes ever on the brink of destitution,

China has no lapsed masses in her teeming cities nor agrarian outrages in her country districts.

There are no socialists and nihilists, nor disputes between labour and capital. This is partly due to the system of government which leaves the highest preferment, actually as well as nominally, open to the son of the day labourer, and partly to their social system and the excellent organisation of their trade unions. Both masters and men are compelled to be members. Non-unionists are not permitted in the trade, and agitators or paid officials would be suppressed by the bamboo. All members of the guild, or union, stand on an equal footing. The guild takes into consideration and adjusts all questions affecting the trade, organises theatricals and processions, and forwards the coffins of deceased members to their ancestral homes. The natives, or descendants of natives of other provinces, residing in a city, of whatever trade, form themselves into a guild. These provincial guilds are often very strong, and may carry an appeal from the local authorities to the viceroy, or even the Emperor himself. Their guild-hall is fitted up as a temple to the tutelary god of their province; the trade-hall, likewise, being a temple to the patron god, or saint, of the trade; and these halls serve besides as council chambers, banqueting rooms, and theatres. Even beggars must join the union, and their dean of guild will undertake to relieve any householder from the visits of the fraternity upon payment of a slump sum by the year. The thieves have also a union, and the list of members is kept by the superintendent of police at the yamen. Any one caught picking and stealing without regularly joining the profession is doubly punished. There is an individual in the district, hand in glove with the police, who insures against larceny for a suitable premium. Every farm house between Ichang and Shasi has his mark on it. When he fails to recover the goods, he pays their value honourably.

Even the magistrates are powerless when the guilds combine against them, and the members of any craft seldom fail to carry their point. Two incidents that came under my observation

may serve to illustrate their tactics. Some boatmen getting into a dispute with steamboat sailors
(native) about the fare were worsted in the melée,
and went and complained to the master of their
guild. Word was immediately passed round that
no boatmen were to load or unload cargo, or take
passengers off and on the steamer, which lay in
the middle of the river, advertised to sail that
evening. Seeing no way out of the difficulty, the
agent had an interview with the headman of the
guild, and business was at once resumed. Chinese
workmen do not quarrel with their rice, and their
demands are generally reasonable.

In the other case a European dismissed five
sawyers engaged by the day to cut wood. On
going in the forenoon to see how the work was
progressing, he found two laths cut, two men
absent, two pretending to adjust the saw, and
the fifth sitting smoking. Indignation got the
better of discretion, and he drove them off the
premises. Next morning he had a new set of
men, but no sooner did one of the old employees
appear upon the scene than they bundled up their

tools and left. After a week spent in the vain endeavour to get other men to do the work, he had no alternative but send for the original five and promise to be more considerate. Had he threatened to deduct from their wages the time he saw them idle he would have come better on, but it saves a world of trouble to contract for piecework.

Workmen never supplant each other, nor do they permit strangers to work in the place until they have joined the local guild; but they have no objection to be under a foreman from a different place, provided he does nothing but superintend and plan. Coolies and boatmen are only allowed to seek employment at their own jetty, where there is a headman to whom the employer makes complaint. Each man, however, makes his own bargain with his employer, and may take more, but dare not take less than the regulation wage. Workmen are seldom troublesome if dealt with fairly and in the right way. When I told them I would not have building operations carried on on Sunday, they never asked a full day's wages, as I expected, but enough to pay for their food. A few of them found a day's work elsewhere, but the majority either visited their friends or went to service. The contractor told me those who rested did better work on the other days. They do not object to do as they are told, however unlike the native methods. Under similar circumstances a European would throw down his tools in disgust; but the Chinese tailor or shoemaker only asks for an old suit of clothes or an old pair of boots, which he carefully takes to pieces, and makes the new according to the pattern.

Scholars are the highest of the four classes into which the people are divided, there being, however, no barrier to prevent passing from one rank to the other. Learned men hold up the light of antiquity to the nation, and are the leaders of society in town and country. The literati and gentry have their own headmen, in addition to those who are over the parish and tything. The nature of their studies has been already indicated, and there is a system of examinations conducted by the Literary Chancellor of the province with a view to promoting learning throughout the empire. The number of students who can at one time obtain the degree of *Siu-tsai* (Budding Genius) is fixed for each district according to population and importance. The distinction consequently implies very different literary attainments in various parts of the country, but the amount of study required is generally equal to what is requisite for a degree at a British University. Fifty or a hundred candidates come forward for every one that can obtain the coveted distinction; but even to pass the preliminaries conveys a certain status. The crowd of competitors includes all ages from fourteen to eighty; and the man who appears regularly at all examinations for sixty years without passing is specially rewarded by the Emperor with the degree of Budding Genius *honoris causa*, parallel to what used to be nicknamed in Scotland "Tombstone Degrees." This is the most honourable distinction that can be acquired at the local centre. After graduating, the literati have to submit to periodical examinations to show that they are not neglecting their books; and if lazy, unruly, or detected assisting litigants, they are stripped of their bachelors' buttons. The button is a knob on the top of a Chinese dress hat, signifying official rank or literary distinction. It is of gold, crystal, red coral, etc., according to the grade.

Most are satisfied with local honours, but the ambitious proceed to the provincial capital with the hope of becoming *Chu-jen*—promoted men. At the provincial examination at Wuchang there will sometimes be 13,000 candidates for the sixty-one degrees allowed triennially to Hupeh. The promoted men are eligible for office, but few obtain it, unless backed by money or influence. About one half of both these degrees are sold by the examiner, and the other half decided by merit. "Money answereth all things," as a very wise Asiatic remarked. Still, merit will come to the front in China. The poor *Chu-jen* may proceed to Pekin and compete for the higher degree of entered scholar. Those who are successful are presented to the Emperor, and immediately receive government employment. There is a still higher examination for the Forest of Pencils, the members of which are enrolled in a sort of Royal Academy and receive salaries from the state. From their numbers, the lowest grade, the budding geniuses, are locally the most influential, and are what is meant by the famous literati of China. The gentry are those who have obtained a similar distinction by their patriotism. When the Peking exchequer is low, its chronic condition, the right to wear a button is conferred upon all who contribute a certain amount to the necessities of the state. It has been as low as ten taels. Along with the empty honour, the wearing of a button secures against the bamboo, when involved in a lawsuit. There are many districts not possessed of half-a-dozen *Chu-jen*, and if a native gains admission to the Forest of Pencils, his name is enrolled in the archives of the city, and certain municipal privileges connected with the Confucian temple are enjoyed for all time by the town.

The second class of the population consists of farmers; and as an honour to their calling and an incentive to industry the Emperor himself holds the plough once a year.

Artizans and labourers who manufacture raw material are the third class. The usual term of apprenticeship is three years, the apprentice eating his master's rice, but receiving no wages. A master tradesman may have six or eight journeymen, occasionally fifty or a hundred; but the methods are primitive, and there is nothing like our factory system. The furniture and implements in common use are clumsily made, but tools often take a fine edge; and, except at places famed for some special manufacture, the processes being traditional in the families that follow the calling, there is no work produced like the curios taken to Europe as samples of Chinese dexterity; yet, an ordinary carpenter or blacksmith is very ingenious, and can imitate European patterns, or work from a picture with a few verbal instructions. Men with a natural turn for mechanics are to be found, who can repair clocks and watches, without ever having learned the trade. Artizans have few tools, and they are mostly unlike ours. Perhaps a blacksmith is the only man who would be at home in a Chinese workshop, and even he would be sorely puzzled with the bellows, which is a long wooden box, constructed on the principle of a syringe with a nozzle at each end, getting a current of air both from the forward and the backward stroke of the piston. His brother artificer, the iron-founder, would be nonplussed by an apparatus so diminutive that blast, furnace, and crucible may all be carried under the arm and set down anywhere in the street by the peripatetic mender of pots and pans.

Craftsmen and labourers are paid about the same rate, not more than from eight pence to a shilling a day. Away from the large treaty ports, where wages are higher, as well as the cost of living, a Chinaman considers himself in a thriving way with twenty-five shillings a month. A budding genius may be engaged

as teacher of the language for very little more.
The Chinese work from daylight to dark seven
days in the week, without more than twenty holidays in the course of the year; but when they are
at their work they do not work nearly so hard
nor yet so steadily as Europeans. The human
frame could not stand it. Of slightly inferior
strength to us, the Chinaman possesses great
endurance, and as stoker of a steamer, or at
other hard work, has no difficulty in taking
turn about with all competitors. Having no
labour saving machinery, the ultimate cost of
production is high. Carpenters' work costs
about the same price as at home, but carving
and ornamental work of all kinds is very much
cheaper. A workman pays two pence halfpenny a day for board, which means boiled
rice and vegetables fried in oil, with a little
fish or pork occasionally. His clothes are
correspondingly cheap, and out of his small
wages he can save a larger proportion than the
British workman can of his. He is fond of
piece-work, when he lays his hands about him

and can earn nearly double the ordinary rate, but the native employer cannot abide the idea of the man that is working to him earning such wages. He thinks he can do better hiring by the day and trusting to his eye and tongue keeping the workman busy.

Traders come last, not as being the least influential, but because they only distribute the fruits of other men's industry, and are not considered so essential to the State. Every Chinaman is a born merchant, and is always ready for a bargain. He is never so happy as when counting money, and the only coinage consisting of brass "cash," strung in hundreds and thousands by a square hole in the centre, twenty-five to thirty being equal to a penny, he finds plenty of this congenial employment. Large sums are paid in silver bullion, weighed in the balance. The "tael," in which Chinese money is reckoned, is not a coin, but a Chinese ounce of silver, equal to an ounce and a third. The fineness, or touch of the silver, which is generally very pure, and the exact weight of the "tael" vary in each dis-

trict.   The rate of exchange between " cash " and
silver is also continually fluctuating, the range in
Ichang being from 1300 to 1560 " cash " per " tael."
Mexican dollars are employed in foreign trade,
but away from the ports they are taken only for
their weight as broken silver. "A shoe " of silver, or
" sycee," as it is technically called, weighs a little
over fifty taels.   There are smaller five and ten
tael pieces.   Small change is procured by cutting
up the larger pieces with a hammer and chisel.
Weights and measures are decimal, with the sole
exception of sixteen *liang*, or " taels," to the *kin*,
or " catty."   One hundred " catties " make a *tan*,
or " picul," equal to 133⅓ pounds.   *Liang*, *kin*,
and *tan* are the Chinese names, the others are
" pidgin," or Canton English, the *lingua franca* of
foreign trade.   " Pidgin " is the nearest approach
that the Chinaman can make to the word business.   Liquids are sold by weight, and grain by
measure.   A Chinaman buys a pound of whisky,
a pint of rice, and a foot of cloth.   The foot contains ten inches, equal to fourteen of ours, but
the exact length varies in different districts and

in different trades. A balance and weights are employed when great accuracy is required, but a Roman steelyard, the beam being made of wood, however, is used for general purposes.

Shops are open in front, and closed at night by heavy wooden shutters, fitted into a groove at the top and bottom. Shopkeepers do not put their names upon their signs, but choose such mottoes as Harmony and Benevolence, a Thousand Profits, Propitious Happiness. As Chinese is read from top to bottom, the carved and gilded sign-boards are suspended vertically, or stuck upright in stone sockets at the shop door. A detailed account is often given on the sign-board of the stock in trade, generally ending with the remark that the goods are genuine and the prices just. Many also exhibit one or other of the following assuring notices:—"One word hall": "No two prices asked": "A child three feet high would not be cheated." The enterprising keeper of an opium den in Ichang displays this legend:—"A sniff of the fragrance would cause a rider to dismount." Chinese shopkeepers make

no secret of the worship of Mammon, for each
shop contains a small shrine to the god of
wealth, and incense is burned at it every morning.   Proverbial wisdom cautions the intending
purchaser to ask the price at three shops, if he
does not want to be cheated.   Every article has
to be bargained for, and the shopman is generally
contented with half he asks.   The following
maxim is to be observed : "When the merchant
asks up to heaven in his price, bid down to earth
in your offer."   A portion of the profit is allowed
to shopmen upon everything they can sell above
the minimum price, which is indicated by a secret
mark.   A customer is frequently called back to
receive the article at his own offer.   Buyers are
careful to guard against mistakes by taking their
own scales and measures along with them.   A
Chinese shopkeeper would be as much surprised
at a customer who did not check the quantity as
at one who did not count the change.

Drafts on any part of China may be obtained
in the large towns, but cheques are not given
in payment of ordinary accounts.   Banks issue

"cash" notes, which are very convenient, as a strong man can only carry about two pounds' worth of the coin of the realm with a yoke over his shoulder. The "cash" notes of a bank have only a local circulation, as their issue is under no sort of control. Any one may start a bank and make paper money, but the difficulty is to find customers and people who will accept the notes. Some banks are very wealthy, but they are of all gradations, down to the man who seats himself at a table in the street, and has no larger negotiations than changing a few dollars into "cash" and cents.

There are no joint-stock companies or Government consols, and almost the only way of investing money is to buy property, lend on mortgage, or open a shop. Merchants frequently pay three per cent. a month as interest, but this exorbitant rate is largely due to the risk of losing both principal and interest. It is often cheaper to lose a debt altogether than to attempt to enforce payment by law, an extreme sample of which I once saw in a landlord sending men to take the roof off a house he had been unfortunate enough to let to a tenant who would neither remove nor pay rent. In a case of bankruptcy each creditor seizes whatever he can lay his hands on. If a man cannot meet his engagements at the Chinese New Year, which is the general money term, his credit is destroyed.

It is a point of honour to keep a bargain. Lose or gain, he will stick to his contract, if he be a decent man. When engaging servants or hiring boatmen or coolies for a journey, the bargain is not binding until they have received a fastening penny. After they have taken their "arles," they may be depended upon, and the man is either very careless or very bad to please who does not find that they serve him well. One may fall into the hands of sharpers, as in other countries, but, generally, if a person treat them justly and show that he knows honest service when he gets it, he will have no reason to complain. They are extremely kind, and never complain for a little extra trouble. I never had anything stolen by servants, boatmen, coolies or inn-keepers. They may take a "squeeze" when they can get it, but I have yet to learn where there is a district in which the stranger is not taken advantage of by the native.

Pawnbroking is a highly respectable vocation, and so universal that the traveller is often left to infer the importance of the town he is coming to by being told the number of pawn shops it contains. Bundles of pawn tickets are always to be seen on the street stalls. Purchasers present the tickets, and on paying the deposit money and the legal interest of one per cent. a month, the pawnbroker is bound to produce the articles and make good any damage they may have suffered in his hands. He has better means of preserving furs and fine cloths than the people generally have themselves, and they are frequently pawned during the summer months as the best way of keeping them. The pawnbroker also keeps a stock of finery to be hired out. Naturally the mandarins pay a good deal of attention to such a thriving industry, and no small portion of their money is invested in banks and pawn shops; not where they hold office, but in their native districts, under the management of brothers and nephews.

The greatest bar to internal trade and social prosperity is the want of good roads, where the waterways are not sufficient. Land transport is by pack-mule, wheelbarrow, and human porterage. The regulation coolie load is eighty catties, one hundred and six pounds and two thirds, to be carried sixty *li*, or twenty miles a day, a very good burden for a man, and it usually exceeds this amount. Coolies in towns carry a picul of one hundred and thirty-three pounds and a third, some taking double loads for double pay. Travelling is done by boat, sedan chair, or on foot. The house boat is very comfortable but slow. Two coolies carry the sedan, but progress is quicker by taking a third man to change. They will cover twenty-five to thirty miles day after day. Every traveller has to take his bedding and other necessaries along with him. The inns on the roads in Central China are wretched, and swarm with vermin. Frequently there is only a small room partitioned off for the inn-keeper and his family, and the remainder of the mud shanty is one large room, kitchen, dining-room, and bedroom. There is one tub in which the coolies wash their feet and the innkeeper washes the dishes, not being too particular about changing the water, and one cloth which serves for all purposes. The traveller takes the door off its hinges and spreads his bedding upon it in the most out of the way corner, and wooes Morpheus with thirty coolies around him, smok-ing opium, gambling, telling stories, or practising on musical (?) instruments. A free fight starts up about midnight, with more high words than bloodshed. The headman makes his appearance before they proceed to extremities.

The peace is wonderfully preserved by these headmen and the system of mutual responsibility for neighbours and kindred. We wait until a person is a criminal before the law steps in, but in China the tything man or the head of a family may complain to the Magistrate about any one under their supervision who is getting into evil

habits and will not take warning.   The mandarin
gives him advice, emphasised in the usual way.
The city guard represses rioting and robbery, but
pays no attention to common brawls, which end
in pulling each other about by the pig-tail, if the
elders cannot adjust them.   As well as the city
gates, which are shut at nightfall, there are barrier
gates across the streets, by which a town is divided
at night into a number of isolated departments.
The carrying of arms is strictly forbidden; and
when out after dark every Chinaman is liable to
arrest who does not carry a lantern with his name
and address conspicuously written upon it.   The
rule is not strictly enforced in peaceful times, but
as there are no street lamps, and the pitfalls are
many in the ill-kept streets, such a lantern is
usually a necessary prevention against broken
bones.   On the outbreak of brigandage, or the
spread of disaffection, every householder has to
exhibit a list of his family at the door, with the
name of any other person who may be staying
with him.   The tything man sees that these lists
are correct, and he may be called upon to compel

one or two able-bodied men, taken in turn from the families under his charge, to watch all night as special constables, armed with short spears. Every Chinaman, upon pain of being considered a rebel, is bound to assist the officers of government in the discharge of their duty. Country districts are patrolled and guarded in the same way as cities: and there existed a system of guard houses and beacons at every five miles along the chief roads, but they have fallen greatly into neglect. By such simple methods the peace is kept, and every man feels that he has a stake in the country, or at least an interest in his town and parish. When he sends his son to school he has placed his foot on the first rung of the ladder that leads to the premiership of the country. A few shillings will buy all the books needed for higher education, and expensive tuition will not help him much. If he has the ability, hard study will land him at the top. I doubt if with all our boards, and elections, and tax-papers, we have much to teach the Chinaman about social order and local government.

The Chinaman never meddles with Imperial politics ; and I have often tried, but always in vain, to explain the British Constitution to a native friend. " So, you elect your own mandarins ; but I suppose they tax you all the same." " Very patriotic of these gentlemen to represent you without being paid for it—but there will be a good many pickings." " Now, really, is that small talk, or are those mandarins at their own expense quite sound in the head ? " or in native phrase, " Are their stomachs good ? " The Chinese always place the seat of intelligence in the gastric region, and not in the brain. " Are their stomachs good, to vex themselves and ruin their families by neglecting their business, all for the public weal ? " Being assured upon this point, he will remark—" A Chinaman is not built that way. What you tell me sounds as strange as the tales in our story-books about the people with square heads, the people with one eye and one leg, those with a hole through their body, and the land where women bear rule, which you laugh at as ridiculous." When sounded on the burning question of the franchise, the Chinaman placidly observes—" The vote! Why should I want a vote? My grandfather never had one, and he was highly respected and lived to an old age."

Such are some of the views I have elicited from my Chinese friends. They and we are cast in a different mould; but in their own way have they not obtained some results that we are still groping after, without any certainty of being on the right track?

CHAPTER VII

THE CHINAMAN AT HOME

THE social unit is the family, and all Chinese
writers maintain that the family must be kept
pure if government is to be just or the country
prosperous. But their views are narrow. In
practice they have improved a little upon Confucius, but they accept his theory. "A woman
can determine nothing of herself, and is subject
to the rule of the three obediences. When young,
she must obey her father and elder brother; when
married, she must obey her husband; when her
husband is dead, she must obey her son. She
may not think of marrying a second time.

176

Woman's business is simply the preparation and supplying of food. Beyond the threshold of her apartments she should not be known for good or evil."

There exists a sentiment, but no law, against the marriage of widows. It is not common among mandarins and the wealthy, but amongst the labouring class is more frequent than among ourselves. Widowhood is an honourable estate. Young widows, or girls whose betrothed husbands have died, are accounted worthy of having special monuments erected to their memory if they decline a second marriage. Specially so if they commit suicide through grief, or if the girl voluntarily goes to wait upon the parents of her betrothed. These monuments to virtuous widows are as highly valued by Chinese families as the right to armorial bearings by our own esquires. In ancestral worship a mother is honoured equally with the father, and the real head of the house is frequently the old grandmother, who seldom fails to rule with a rod of iron. A man would be ashamed to be seen

M

walking in the street with his wife, but he will support his mother on his arm.

Polygamy exists in a modified form. A man can have but one legal wife, but he may have as many concubines as he pleases. They are simply slaves, the servants of their mistress, who is the mother of their children in the eye of the law. All the children have equal privileges. These secondary unions are supposed to be promoted by the wife, if she have no son to perpetuate the family and keep up the ancestral worship, but she generally prefers to find a way out of the difficulty by adopting a nephew of her husband. The mass of the people are monogamists, and many officials have but one wife. Others freely avail themselves of the liberty allowed, and incur no odium by so doing. The emperor is the only person whose position renders a plurality of wives imperative.

Divorce is very loose, but the principal or secondary wife who has borne a son to her husband cannot be put away. There is a provision by which a man may send his wife to the magistrate to be disposed of to the highest bidder if she proves unsatisfactory.   At Ichang I never knew of its being resorted to except by a few peasants.   These "mandarin beauties" are on show at the yamen, but do not command a large price.   There is a proverb that a good husband will not beat his wife, but there is no protection against that or other forms of cruelty, and the alarming number of female suicides is an index of the misery that exists in the inner apartments. It is, however, generally the mother-in-law and not the husband who is blamed, and Chinese will commit suicide for very trivial causes.   It is the resort of the apprentice who is detected pilfering from his master; and when a man can find no other way of being revenged on his enemy he goes and commits suicide on his doorstep with the idea that his ghost will haunt him.

It is rare to meet with women who can read and write, and as one distinguished native author pleads for the extension of female education with the argument that even white mice may be taught to turn a wheel, it may be inferred

that the blue-stocking is non-existent, and her
advent undreamt of. Women attend to household duties, and are not denied a voice in
domestic affairs. Young ladies are kept in
strict seclusion, but all women are freely allowed
to visit each other, the well-to-do riding in
curtained sedan chairs, and the wives of poor
people enjoy about as much liberty as elsewhere. The members of a family usually take
their meals together, but females do not sit with
male visitors; nor is it proper to take any notice
of them, should they happen to pass through
the room where guests are seated. In the "inner
apartments" it does not appear necessary to dis-
semble and pretend to such indifference. The
European visitor, at any rate, speedily sees
numerous holes being made in the paper covered
lattices that serve as windows, with wet finger
tips, and eager almond-shaped dark eyes peering
through, presumably belonging to the "pearls"
within. Women are not exactly badly used,
but they are treated as inferiors, and regarded
with none of those tender and chivalrous feelings

which are the outcome of Christianity. One rarely sees them doing anything beyond their strength, or unsuited to their sex. The Hakka women, however, are an exception. The coolie's wife has her silk dresses and jewelry of gold and silver. Female clothes are all tailor made. In poor families women do the cooking, but bestow little care in keeping their houses tidy. When washing, they sit down on a stool and hammer the clothes on a big stone. They spend a great deal of time gossiping and smoking tobacco, which is used by all, male and female.

Marriage is a duty, which nothing but poverty can excuse in a man, and as for the ladies, suitors are so plentiful that all are married. There are no old maids, and no name for them in the language. Girls usually marry from fifteen to eighteen, and boys from seventeen to twenty. The infant mortality is great, and I never knew a Chinese family of my acquaintance in which ten children attained the age of twenty. They also age more rapidly than we do. Near relatives and people of the same surname are forbidden to marry. The parties concerned have no choice of their partners in life, all being arranged by their parents, with the aid of go-betweens. Betrothals frequently take place in childhood. An astrologer is employed to cast the horoscope of the two young people, and it having been ascertained that the " doors match," slips of red paper, on which are written eight characters, giving the names and nativities of the bride and bridegroom are interchanged. After this, the marriage engagement cannot be broken off. Either party may turn cripple or blind, or the boy may grow up a worthless young man, or his family sink into poverty ; still there is no escape for the bride. The bridegroom is not supposed to see her face until the marriage ceremony is over, and he lifts the bridal veil of red cloth. Deceptions as gross as Laban's are easily and frequently practised. Parents do not part with their daughters without a substantial sum of money to compensate in part for their up-bringing, and the bride never has a dowry. The bridegroom has also to make

her presents of clothes and jewelry. He is a
lucky man if a year's wages enable him to do
all this; but he would manage to get a widow
at half the outlay. The natives estimate the
prosperity of the times by the rise and fall of
the matrimonial market.

There are many diverse marriage customs, but
the legal part consists in the interchange of the
" eight characters," followed by the home-taking
of the bride. The bride is carried to her future
home upon the marriage day in a red sedan chair,
never used on other occasions, accompanied by a
band of music and the discharge of fire-crackers.
The bride and bridegroom take a sip of wine out
of the same cup, and kneel together before the
bridegroom's parents and the ancestral tablets of
the family. The newly married couple sit side
by side at the marriage feast, but custom does
not permit the bride to eat anything. After it is
over she is placed in the corner of a room, into
which men and women crowd indiscriminately,
and her small feet, the size of which is the great
test of female beauty, are placed on a footstool for

general admiration. Any passer by may go in and have a look at the bride's feet. She is made the butt of ridicule and the object of coarse and ribald jests, in which her own sex are foremost. Trying as the ordeal must be, the bride would consider herself and her family disgraced were any part omitted, and the fun goes on fast and furious the whole night long.

Foot-binding is a painful and tedious process, inflicted in childhood. The small toes are bent in succession under the sole of the foot, and kept in position by tight bandages. Then the bandages are so applied that the foot is broken at the instep and pressed downwards, whilst the heel, which is greatly elongated, is pressed downwards and forwards. The weight rests on the point of the great toe and the heel, the total length of the foot being three or four inches, and a fine lady's shorter. The use of the ancle joint is lost; the muscles of the ball waste away; and the vitality of the whole limb below the knee is lowered, and it becomes subject to obstinate sloughing ulcers. The general health suffers less than might be supposed from this barbarous metamorphosis of the human foot into a "golden lily." The use of tight bandages can never be dispensed with in after life, and the attempt to let the foot resume its natural shape is as painful as the original process. The custom is enforced neither by law nor religion, but solely by fashion. Its origin is obscure, but it has not prevailed for more than a thousand years. The story is that the ladies of the imperial harem first commenced it in imitation of the club feet of a favourite concubine, her deformity being supposed to be the source of attraction. The example of their Manchu rulers, whose women have large feet, has not produced the slightest effect upon the Chinese. On the conquest of the country the Manchus compelled the men to shave their heads and adopt the pigtail, it being the custom previously to wear the hair long tied up in a top-knot, like the Taoist priests. They also succeeded in making them wear the Tartar dress instead of the old national costume, but they utterly failed to alter female fashion, an edict against foot-binding having had to be rescinded. In some parts small feet betoken wealth, or at least a striving after gentility, but in many districts both rich and poor are compelled to submit to it, large feet being a mark of prostitution.

Female infanticide is so prevalent in some districts that a fourth of the female children are estimated to be destroyed, but at other places, as at Ichang, it scarcely appears to be more common than we might expect it to be among a heathen people. There are, however, multitudes of female slaves, brought chiefly from the province of Sz-chuan. The girls are sold by their parents, and are recognised articles of commerce, paying duty at the native custom-houses. I have frequently seen a child of three or four hawked in the streets for sale by its father. Female slaves act as domestic servants, and are generally well treated, public opinion compelling their owners to see them married at a suitable age, when they become possessed of all the rights of ordinary Chinese women. They are often bought as secondary wives, and thrifty parents frequently purchase girls with the express purpose of bringing them up and marrying them to their sons, a cheap method of settling them in life. This is, however, but one side of female slavery. There are many speculators who bring up girls and traffic in them for vice.

Sons inherit in equal portions and daughters get nothing, as they pass into the family of their husbands. There is little power of making a will. The law of inheritance is influenced by their peculiar family life. Not only does the bride enter the family of her husband's father and become practically the servant of her mother-in-law, but it is considered very commendable for the members of a family to continue to live together after their parents' death. Even when the establishment of separate households becomes a desideratum for the sake of peace, they often preserve the family property intact, and divide the rent or produce.

So long as his father is alive a man is a minor, and cannot marry or engage in business against his wish. A father may beat his son as he pleases; he may carry off his goods or lift his wages; he may contract debt and send the creditors to his son for payment of the account. Chinese parents generally spoil their children when young, and beat them unmercifully when they get old enough to be mischievous.

Their system of reckoning kinship is more complete than ours. There are different names for brothers and sisters as they happen to be older or younger than the speaker, different names for uncles and aunts as they are on the father's or mother's side, and a distinction is drawn amongst cousins as they come through the male and female, or elder and younger branches of the family. No European pretends to be thoroughly up in the scheme of Chinese relationship.

Chinese names are nearly as puzzling. Every man has a surname, or clan name, which never changes, unless by adoption or by entering the Buddhist priesthood, when he drops it. But he has a milk name, a family name, a literary name, and so on. When a bachelor obtains his degree

he takes a new name.   The milk names are such
as Beggar, Board, or Autumn Kid.   One of my
friends called his son Thirty-Nine.   That was
not his position in the family, but the age of the
happy father.   They have the idea that the gods
will not send sickness on beggars or autumn
kids.   When children fall sick they dress them
as Buddhist priests to conciliate the deities, or
put a collar round their necks and call them pigs
or puppies to cheat them.   They have no names
like John or Thomas, but when they attain man-
hood choose such flowery designations as Golden
Mountain, Pervading Principle, Approaching
Happiness.   They put these names on their
visiting cards, which are of red paper the size
of an octavo page, but do business under their
shop name, or "chop."   Ladies are usually
named after flowers.   Common people are ad-
dressed as Teacher, officials as Old Grandfather
or Excellency.

A Chinaman's house is a very cheerless abode,
and they have no good equivalents for *home* or
comfort.   He feels most at ease in a dark corner.

I once engaged a coolie to take care of an empty house, and on going to see that everything was correct, saw no sign of bedding, and suspected he might be spending his nights elsewhere, but he set my mind at rest by pointing out his quarters in a dark hole under the stair, which he had selected as the most comfortable apartment in the house. If the passengers on a river steamer can gain admission to the hold, they take up their quarters above the cargo in preference to occupying the comfortable and airy cabins on deck.

The ordinary workman's house is a cabin of mud or sun-dried bricks roofed with thatch, without window or chimney. The poorest prefer to have the kitchen outside, though it be only a piece of matting to keep off the sun and rain. Many live in tenements of bamboo mats, or reeds plastered with mud. The better class of houses are built of burnt bricks and roofed with small tiles. Both bricks and tiles are a dark bluish grey. Stones are used for the foundation, but not for building the walls, however good and plentiful they may be. The bricks are very thin, and are laid on the flat and set on edge alternately, forming a hollow wall with binders at every layer. The walls could not support the roof, which rests on wooden pillars, but if well pointed or plastered and securely coped to keep out the rain, they last for a long time. Builders commence by raising the frame-work and putting on the roof; the walls are added as an afterthought. There is a large ornamental gateway with a heavy wooden door in front; then usually a small courtyard before coming to the house proper, the outer walls of which are not relieved by a single window. The peculiar slope of the roof and ornamental turned up corners indicate the Tartar tent as the original model of the Chinese architect. Light and air in such moderate quantities as a Chinaman cares for, are admitted by the heavenly well, a portion of the roof left uncovered. Right at the back of it is the guest-hall, the principal room of the house. Bedrooms and private apartments are ranged along the

sides of the guest-hall, and derive a dim and
uncertain light through frames of lattice work,
covered with paper. The internal partitions are
made of wood, with curtains for doors. Large
houses contain suite after suite of rooms stretching backwards, with more heavenly wells to
admit light. Great expense may be incurred
in carving and gilding, but there are rarely
wooden floors to any of the rooms, and never
carpets. A second or third story may be added
in crowded towns, but an ordinary house is all
on the ground floor. It is as cold inside as in
the open air, and although charcoal chafing
dishes are used for the hands and feet, the
main dependence for warmth is placed upon
robe above robe, lined with fur or quilted with
cotton. The soles of the boots are an inch
thick and composed of felt and paper, good
non-conductors. Draughty and damp and cold
as their houses are, the Chinese are not excessively afflicted with coughs. A native house
is cool in summer, but intolerably stuffy and
malarious.

The furniture is ponderous, square, and uncomfortable.   The chairs are straight-backed,
angular, and never upholstered, although a small
hard cushion is placed upon them occasionally.
A row of small tea-tables and chairs is placed
along either side of the guest-hall, and at the
further end a daïs for the honoured guests.
Above it is a shrine with the ancestral tablets,
family idols, and a few vases and other curios.
The guest-hall serves as dining and drawing-
room.   Its walls are ornamented with drawings
and scrolls inscribed with maxims from the
classics, and antithetical couplets.   The honoured
guest is seated at the upper end, on the left
hand of the host, who informs the visitor that
he expects great felicity to rest upon his dwelling
since he is thus honoured by a call.   Instead of
shaking hands, a Chinaman clasps his own before
his breast and makes a low obeisance.   To one
much his superior he goes on his knees and
knocks his head on the ground.   He does not
ask if you are well, but whether you have eaten
your rice.   Having rice and a good appetite,

you ought to be thankful. The weather is not the universal topic of conversation. Your host, or even a casual acquaintance, takes a kindly interest in your welfare. He asks your honourable name, how old you are, how many children you have, if your parents be alive, what is your occupation, where you have come from, and whither you are going. To omit any of these queries upon introduction to him would be excessively rude, and a plain hint that he did not wish to cultivate your acquaintance. From rich or poor you are offered the same tokens of civility, a pipe of tobacco and a cup of tea. Manners are taught at school, and a Chinaman is always polite and never flurried. All classes have the same etiquette, and a labourer receives you in his mud cabin with the grace and ease of a courtier. He can be rude enough when he likes, but he never is a clumsy bumpkin.

In the dim and uncertain light of a Chinese bedroom, we see that the walls are bare, the floor unswept, and the roof garnished with cobwebs. A bed, a couple of old chairs, a few boxes, a small press, and perhaps a washstand, constitute the furniture. In the north they sleep on platforms heated by flues, but elsewhere the bedstead consists of a few boards placed on trestles, or is a huge poster of the box pattern. Mattresses are dispensed with, and their place supplied by a layer of straw with a quilt spread over it. Quilts take the place of blankets, and sheets are little used. The covers can be taken off the quilts and washed, but it is not done very often. The pillows are small and hard, and placed under the back of the neck. Wrapped in Chinese quilts, a European may sleep in an open shed, or under a mat in a boat, when snow is on the ground, without any bad effect. In summer a Chinaman often takes a small form into the street and sleeps on it, poised on his back, with no covering but a pair of short cotton trousers.

He does without neckties, cuffs, collars, and starched linen. His shirt and drawers are shaped exactly like his jacket and trousers. In warm weather he wears no other clothes indoors, but he puts on a long gown of silk, blue calico, or white

grass cloth, when he goes out. As the cold
increases, he puts on a greater number of wadded
jackets, and cases his legs in wadded leggings.
His stockings are made of white calico, with the
seams so hard and uncomfortable that a taste is
spreading for foreign socks. The Chinese are
fond of flannel for underclothing, and could our
manufacturers instruct them in the way of washing it, they would buy large quantities.

Ladies' garments are very similar to the male
attire. Their loose jacket is longer than that of
the men, but they never wear the long gown.
In some districts the wearing of a plaited skirt
over the trousers is common, but at Ichang it is
only done by the common people upon grand
occasions. Neither men nor women go bare-
footed, even the coolie has a pair of straw sandals,
and others always stockings and shoes. The
ladies' toilet is elaborate, and contains no mystery,
as women of the poorer class perform it for each
other in the street. The hair is combed back
and fixed in a chignon, being stiffened by an
application of the glutinous water in which rice is

boiled. Artificial or real flowers and jewelled head ornaments are freely used. Unengaged girls wear their hair in a pig-tail like the boys, tied with red instead of black braid. Engaged young ladies put theirs up in a chignon, and married women pull out the short hair round the temples. They all paint, but there is no secret about it, and the men admire it.   The face is rubbed over with sugar and water, then thickly dusted with white powder. The cheeks and lips are painted with vermilion, and the eyebrows darkened with charcoal.   A lady's toilet is too elaborate to be performed every day, and the small pillow preserves the coiffure. Few of either sex are free from vermin.

The Chinese are partial to soups and stews. The meat is cut into small pieces convenient for the chopsticks, and soup eaten with a porcelain spoon. The thorough cooking which meat undergoes, often in boiling oil or lard, is the only explanation I can suggest for the immunity with which they eat dead animals and all sorts of carrion. Their cookery is quite one of the fine

arts, but they use too much grease and garlic, and
the ingredients are of too doubtful origin, to make
it tempting to Europeans. When Chinese entertain
their friends, they usually bargain with the keeper
of an eating-house to provide so many tables. The
tables are square and seat two persons at each
side, but whatever be the number at a table the
same quantity of food is served. There is no
table-cloth, and bones are thrown on the floor.
Each person is provided with a pair of chopsticks,
a porcelain spoon, a small wine cup, and one or
two diminutive saucers for sauce. Everything is
arranged in perfect order upon the polished table,
the centre of which is occupied by nine dishes
containing fruit and sweetmeats. As many tables
are spread as the number of guests demands.
When all are seated a kettle of hot spirits is
brought in, and they pledge each other. The
appetite is next whetted by roasted melon seeds,
sugar candy, and such like. The guests put in
their handkerchiefs whatever of the dessert they
do not eat, and when the table is cleared, the
substantial part of the repast is ushered in by a

stewed crab being placed upon the table. Then
comes a succession of fish, flesh, and fowl, swim-
ming in fat, and eaten without bread or rice; but
mushrooms and vegetables and pastry enter into
the composition of many of the dishes. Less
than nine of such courses is not counted respectable, and I have sat from four o'clock in the
afternoon till ten at night, and finally had to
succumb, without seeing any appearance of the
end. The kettle of spirits circulates freely and
tobacco pipes are handed round. As they warm
to the work, the chopsticks (lit. nimble boys)
are plied with such vigour that the guests cast
their coats. Everything is paid for, eaten or not,
and the host feels flattered by the voraciousness
of his friends; and the loudness of their eructations *BELCHES*
bears evidence to their inward satisfaction. They
play a game of forfeits by suddenly throwing out
the fingers from the closed hand, the opponent
endeavouring to guess the number they fall short
of ten, before he has had time to count. The
loser is compelled to drink a cup of spirits. The
dinner is brought to an end by a small basin of

plain boiled rice being handed to each guest, and
tea is brought in and cloths wrung through warm
water to wipe the hands.   All lift the pieces
of food out of the same centre dish with their
chopsticks, and help each other to the daintiest
morsels.   A guest may leave at any time by
rising from the table, bowing to the host, and
declaring that he can eat no more.   In any case,
all take their departure as soon as the meal is over.

Chinese wine is fermented and distilled from
grain, usually tall millet.   The vine is indigenous
to the country, but they do not make grape wine.
There are many varieties of this "samshu," varying greatly in strength.   The common sort is a
clear, coarse whisky, which is very potent, and
has a maddening effect on any sailors who may
be tempted to try it from its cheapness.   There is
no restriction on its sale or manufacture, and a
bottle may be bought for twopence.   Most
Chinese take a little with every meal, but never
at any other time.   They are a sober people, and
in all probability we should be the same, if whisky
were so cheap and common that it was no treat

to offer it to any one. Tea is the liquor offered to visitors at all hours of the day. The cup is small, and there is neither sugar, milk, nor cake along with it. The cup is replenished as it is emptied, but to call the servant to bring in fresh tea, is a polite hint to the guest to leave. A liking for the infusion of the sun-dried leaf is readily acquired, and there is no drink safer or more refreshing in hot weather.

The water is bad, and cannot be used without boiling. Wells and springs are worse than the rivers, in which the impurity is chiefly mud, which falls to the bottom of the vessel on the addition of a little alum. The Chinese are quite alive to the deleterious qualities of cold water, which they set down to its coldness and rawness. They suppose it to require cooking like everything else. They drink only hot tea, and wash and bathe in warm water. The detestable character of the water must be due to organic matter to excess in the soil. At any rate, an incautious draught from a clear spring is very apt to cause diarrhœa.

The Chinese have always been a people given to ceremony, and they flatter themselves that they have a monopoly of good breeding. Not many would sit down to their correspondence without a copy of the complete letter-writer at their elbow, from which they may cull the phrases appropriate to every occasion. The personal pronouns are only used between intimate friends, or to persons much inferior to the speaker. A Chinaman would take great offence at being told he was awkward in his manner or blunt in his speech, but is not disconcerted in the slightest by an expression of your conviction that he is deviating from the truth. He compliments you on your shrewdness, to throw you off your guard, and starts off with a fresh string of fabrications. If you manifest any sign of annoyance it is an evidence of your "barbarity." All this is as it should be. The hero of a Chinese novel is praised when he prevents unseemly disclosures by telling lies all round.

The Chinaman contrives to get much enjoyment at a cheap rate. He does not concern himself with anything but his immediate surroundings, but in his own circle, he always knows the latest gossip, and is intimately acquainted with his neighbour's affairs. Tea-shops take the place of newspapers ; the temple and the theatre are both free and open ; and there is generally something lively in the magistrate's court. There are periodical festivals with processions and illuminations, the annual dragon-boat races, the New-Year holidays, changes of magistrates, army reviews, executions, and official proclamations. Little interest is manifested in suicides and boat accidents, for human life is cheap ; but the fullest details of the latest ghost are eagerly inquired after, the recent portent in the sky is discussed, and half-a-day is profitably spent at anytime getting circumstantial accounts of the baby that has been born with a head three times as large as its body. The Chinaman is not a loafer, but he is seldom in a hurry, and is never taciturn. The triennial examinations come round, and everybody has an interest in some of the competitors. Street porters discuss the theme prescribed for yesterday's essay, and when the list of successful candidates is posted up, there is as great a crowd and as much excitement as when the result of a contested election is declared. Copies are hastily printed off, and hawked through the streets at midnight.

The active sports of Europeans are a puzzle to the natives. Lawn tennis never fails to attract a crowd of spectators at every coign of vantage, and it is amusing to mix with the onlookers and hear their speculations as to the amount of the stakes that could induce well-to-do people to exert themselves so violently. When the game was introduced to Ichang I had some difficulty in persuading my native friends that the British Consul and Commissioner of Customs had not discovered a new and fascinating mode of gambling. The Shanghai races are celebrated throughout the eighteen provinces, and on approaching a remote hamlet the street gamins have occasionally saluted me, not with the familiar "Beat the foreign devil," but with a

gleesome shout, " His excellency has come to
establish horse races." The Chinese practise
archery a little as a pastime, but no one shoots
or fishes for sport. Old and young amuse themselves by taking out their cages and singing birds
when they go for an evening stroll on the city
wall. Graybeards fly kites—but it requires some
skill to fly a Chinese dragon-kite, composed of a
hundred pieces. Dandies disport themselves as
elsewhere, although there be no ladies abroad to
admire the spectacle, upsetting the theory that
the dude is a bye-product of the coquette. They
pride themselves on the elegance of their long
robes, the length of their finger nails, which be-
tokens them to be above the necessity of manual
labour, their jade bracelets, the grace with which
they manipulate their fans, and the size of their
spectacles, which indicates studious habits. They
affect the slow and grave demeanour of the sage,
and are at great pains to make themselves appear
older than they are. Age is honour in China.
All carry pocket mirrors, which they use in
public, and if they can grow a few hairs, rather

a difficult thing to do upon Mongolian lips, they wear a moustache comb at the button hole of their jacket. A moustache may be grown at forty, and a beard at sixty; not sooner, unless the wearer has official rank.

The Punch and Judy show is indigenous to China, and there is no want of jugglers, acrobats, peep-show men, wandering musicians and story tellers. Instead of waiting until the end, the street artiste sends round the hat about the middle of his performance when it is at the most interesting part, and if the coppers are not forthcoming, decamps for a fresh pitch. Boys whip their tops, play hop-scotch, and kick their shuttlecocks. Quack doctors are numerous, extolling the virtues of their pills and plasters. The spectacled gentleman seated at a small table with writing materials before him will write a letter, draw out a deed of sale, cast a horoscope, or write a charm with equal facility. Blind men scrape on a fiddle to call the attention of the perplexed, whose doubts they will resolve; for, having lost their natural vision, they can see into the future. Beggars and priests solicit alms, and both promise a liberal recompense in the future world. Hucksters, fruit-sellers, travelling barbers, portable cook-shops, sedan chairs, loaded coolies, the retinue of mandarins, pack mules, and wheelbarrows crowd the narrow street, which has no side walks. All struggle for a passage with each other and the swarms of pigs and pariah dogs. If there be any attempt at sanitation it is in the form of a deep ditch in the centre of the street, covered with rough flag stones, having holes between the joinings that would admit the foot of the unwary. The sewers are always choked, and every house has a receptacle for preserving whatever is valuable as manure; yet the population flourishes and increases in defiance of the laws of health. Cholera and other epidemics are, however, seldom absent from the towns, but a few sporadic cases occasion no alarm. When very prevalent, they endeavour to drive off the demons that cause the disease. During an epidemic at Ichang the Brigadier-General marched the troops to man the city walls morning and evening, and striking up the gongs and drums, kept them firing blank shot at the invisible foe for an hour at a time.

Chess is a great indoor pastime. The board, pieces, and moves are all peculiar. Dice, cards, and dominoes are implements of gambling, also taking up a handful of peas and guessing the number, odd or even. The dice and dominoes are similar to ours, but the cards are quite different. Their games require no skill. A Chinese gambler trusts to his luck and not his play. Grasshoppers are caught in the season and made to fight. The creatures fly at each other like cocks, and large sums are staked upon the event. The spirit of gambling is so strong that men frequently lose everything they possess, and a school boy prefers trying his luck to buying a farthing's worth of sweets. Gambling is punishable by law, but no legislation can put it down.

Learned men are supposed to pass their dignified leisure in friendly contests at composing verses. But it is to be feared the dice-box and the opium pipe and the latest scandal are as attractive to them as to the vulgar. They may, however, frequently be seen admiring specimens of good hand-writing with the æsthetic fervour of Western connoisseurs dwelling upon statuary and painting. They read very little as an amusement or recreation. The literature is not enticing. A novel in twenty-four volumes is hardly light reading. Their standard encyclopædia, recently reprinted in Shanghai in six hundred volumes, is warranted to contain no article which is not five hundred years old. Far be it from me to cast doubt on the elegance of Chinese literature—and the elegance of an essay counts for much more than its matter—but it is not interesting, and seems intended for readers who expected to attain the age of the antediluvians.

The "stupid people," which is the fatherly term constantly employed in official proclamations for those who do not come under the headings of literati, gentry, and soldiers, often amuse themselves by asking riddles. There is a jar with three mouths, full all day and empty all night. *Ans.* A pair of trousers. There is a gentleman with a red head, who sings when he goes and is silent when he sits. *Ans.* A blue-bottle fly. It will follow you for a thousand miles, but will not enter a house with you. *Ans.* Your shadow. An emperor all day and a beggar at night. *Ans.* A play-actor. Plays are always performed by daylight, and the profession of an actor is disreputable; whereas it is shrewdly surmised that the beggar, who is misery itself on his daily round, is often fairly comfortable when his work is over.

The Chinese are artistic in their tastes, but fine art does not exist. It has never got beyond the stage of decoration. Their perspective is very defective, and they usually dispense with shade, holding it to be due to defect of vision. They will draw and colour the petals of a flower or the wing of a butterfly with perfect accuracy, but they cannot compose a picture. Their statuary is worse than their painting; and in both they succeed best with the quaint and grotesque, and fail most lamentably with the pathetic and sublime. In jewelry and ivory carving they display good taste and excellent workmanship. In speaking of Chinese art, it must be remembered that their artists are only journeymen tradesmen, who have received no special training, and are paid but ordinary tradesmen's wages. Under the circumstances their performances are worthy of all praise.

Music is a necessary part of all ceremonies. Confucius ascribed to it the power of reforming the moral nature. It must have deteriorated since his time, for that is anything but the effect it now produces. Their scale is different from ours, and the performers seem to foreign ears merely to vie with each other in producing the greatest volume of discordant noise. The national instrument is the gong, but they have a great variety of drums, cymbals, flutes, clarionets, guitars, and violins. The *la-pa* produces a sound exactly the same as the bagpipe chanter.

Gambling and sensuality are the great vices of the Chinese, the latter taking unnatural forms with terrible frequency. They are not more deceitful than other Asiatics, but appear to have greater boldness and success in practising their tricks upon Europeans. They are adepts at faking up antiques and curios. Very few ever visited China without having some story to tell of buying boiled rice for carved ivory, or such like. There is but one way of avoiding being cheated at times—never buy. Opium smoking is on all fours with whisky drinking. The "opium ghost" I know to be quite as bad as the alcoholic wreck, despite a hundred blue-books to the contrary. I am also aware that nearly every Chinaman at Ichang indulges in a little opium about the New Year and other high occasions; yet there is no sign of the people being poisoned wholesale. But no Chinaman ever defends opium on moral, and very seldom upon medical grounds, as a cure for consumption or antidote to ague. The seller of it will tell you that it pays, and the smoker that he likes it, but both admit that it is an expensive luxury and an insidious foe, which a man is very much better without.

CHAPTER VIII

THE CHINAMAN REFLECTED IN HIS OWN MIRROR

Proverbs—Obiter dicta—A last word.

"THE man who has read the Tseng-Kwang (a collection of proverbs) knows how to converse;" but it is not to improve our talking powers that I now refer to the hoary compilation, but because a Chinaman ever seasons his discourse with ancient saws which throw a more accurate light upon his character than any analysis by an outsider.

"Customs vary in every place, but there is no place like home." "Chang-an may be a fine city, but it will not do for a permanent residence." "Life and death depend on fate, and wealth and poverty on the will of Heaven." "Disease may be cured, but not luck." It is many a one's lot to have "An ambitious heart and an obscure destiny." "The lucky man always gets a fair wind"; yet to all who will seize fortune at the flood, "A day will come for threshing corn" (in the open air). "When you see an opportunity, act." "It is vain to lament after you have missed your chance," for "Peaches only blossom in the second month, and chrysanthemums in the ninth." Do not be too ambitious; "If you cannot hook fish, you may net shrimps."

"A good work was never done without much trouble." "It is better to go home and make a net than go to the river and wish for fish." "If you strike a flint you will get fire," but "It sometimes thunders loudly and brings little rain." "By perseverance you may grind an iron anchor into a needle." If you can do that, and "Live on cabbage shanks," you will accomplish anything. But there are absolute impossibilities, such as "To force a hen to hatch chickens," or "To see the hairs on the back of your neck," or "To cook without rice."

"By careful reflection all things grow easy," but "What is done hastily is done badly." Too many affairs are " Like gourds in a tub of water one pops up while you press another down." " Seven hands and eight feet " would be embarrassing superfluities, and " Eight pilots and seven sailors " do not facilitate navigation. " Each man to his trade " ; " Beat your own gong and sell your own candy." " The schoolmaster should stick to his books, the crofter look after his pigs, the priest go to the monastery, and the merchant to his shop." " A man of many trades can never bring up his family." A Chinaman is very ingenious, but he will " Never attempt what is not in his line." " A bad cook will spoil a good dinner."

" There are three rules for men in office : be upright, be cautious, be diligent." The pity is that " An honest magistrate cannot thrive." " Of ten reasons for which a magistrate decides a case, nine are not made public." " Neither dogs nor mandarins injure those who give them anything." " Deceive, but do not insult a mandarin." " The court-house is a deep pit." " The mandarin will not pity your poverty, nor the devil your leanness." "If a word gets into court, nine bullocks cannot pull it out." "Win your lawsuit, and lose your money." "A cow goes amissing while you are catching a cat." "The dignity of office is widely known," but there exists a providence whereby, "When the Emperor wishes a minister to die, he dies."

"To catch the big penny you must let the little penny go." "When taken in, say nothing about it." "Do not buy everything that is cheap," but try to "Make every penny serve two purposes." "Twenty per cent. on ready money is better than thirty on credit." A man in debt is "Like a frog at the bottom of a well." Avoid lending your name, for "If you stand security for the bow, you will be held responsible for the arrow." "When you visit the pawnshop, say nothing about it." "Those who are doing a good trade never grudge the taxes." "Who would rise early if he saw no profit?"

"Among a hundred men you will find all kinds and colours." "The present age is not to be compared to antiquity." "Good men are scarce."

Some are " Lying machines," with " The skin of
the face as thick as a wall," and " Black hearts
and rotten livers." " There are only two good
men ; one is dead, and the other not born." " A
clever man understands a nod," but "A conceited
man makes many mistakes." " Good men suffer
much." " They err greatly who will not take an
old man's advice." There are " Wolves in the
skins of sheep " even in China. Some men have
" Two tongues in one mouth." Others are stupid,
"Wooden men," mere "Leather lanterns." Worse
still, some are " Lumps of dregs," " Thick enough
to make porridge," " Unmindful of all the eight "
things which a Chinaman should practise. In
short, "Man is heaven and earth in miniature."

" Never say brother-in-law to a Buddhist
priest," since he cannot lawfully marry. " Never
quarrel with a woman." " Do not provoke mandarins, customers, or widows." " Nine women in
ten are jealous," and "Nothing will frighten a wilful
wife but a beating." Conjugal felicity is not unknown. Then, " The husband sings and the wife

rejoices." In any case, "It is better to be a poor man's bride than a rich man's concubine."

"Parents do not see their children's faults"; true all the world over. "Brothers are like hands and feet." "Though the left hand overcome the right, no advantage is gained." Still, "Brothers keep separate money accounts." "A tried friend is a treasure," but some friendships are such miserable affairs as the alliance between "The scraper of an opium pipe and the potsherd" on which it is cleaned. "Friends over meat and drink, husband and wife whilst rice and fuel last." The three great vices are, "Lechery, gambling, and opium smoking." "The truth is another name for stupidity."

"The poorer one gets, the more devils he meets." "The poor have peace when the rich have trouble." "The man who makes a fortune by roguery will not enjoy it long." "Money covers many offences," but "The rich can no more suppress the village guilds than the mountains can cover the sun." "If poor, do not lose your self-reliance, and if rich, do not act like a fool." Honest poverty is no disgrace, for " The Son of Heaven has straw-sandalled relations."

" Those who lay up goodness enjoy happiness ; those who lay up evil suffer grief." " Virtue has its reward, and vice its punishment, although re- tribution may be long delayed." Very good ; but there is another proverb, " If you talk of con- science, you will have nothing to eat."

" Man's life is a stage-play." " Man's life is like a candle in the wind or hoar-frost on the tiles." " What centenarian had 36,000 days of pleasure ? " " It is a light thing to starve to death, but a serious matter to lose one's virtue." " When the general's wife dies, a hundred visitors come to condole with him ; but when he dies himself, not a single soldier goes into mourning." " You may get another wife, but not another mother." " Any kind of life on earth is better than being under the ground."

Religion is at a low ebb and its ministers de- spised. " The priest can read his missal, but he does not understand it." " Each day's mass costs three taels" (ten to twelve shillings). " Only those become priests who can make a living at nothing else." "The cottage with its bamboo grove is pleasanter than the monastery." "The monastery faces the nunnery; there is nothing in that." "Three strokes of the axe will make an image of Yang-sz" (the god of sailors). "It is superfluous to put a beard on Yang-sz," who is always represented as a youth. "To bathe an idol, is to put his godship to needless inconvenience." "You need not go and pray in the temple, if you neglect the two Buddhas at home," your father and mother. "Though you do not believe in the other gods, you must believe in Lei-Kung," the god of thunder. "To be struck by lightning is a visible punishment." All Chinese believe this, and hold that it is a fate which only overtakes the very wicked. "You may deceive men, but you cannot deceive the gods." If this be their belief, they do not act upon it, and another proverb is more descriptive of their practice. "The stinking pig's head is good enough to set before the smelless idol." "Better do a kindness at home than go on a pilgrimage." "When you have done your duty, abide by the will of Heaven."

The above are a few specimens of thousands of proverbs in daily use by the Chinese. Many of the most pointed have been omitted on account of their vulgarity. Those given have been well-nigh selected at random, but they may serve to illustrate various phases of the Chinese mind and character. They are not a people to be delineated in a few sentences, and those who know them best are the slowest to make general statements or predict the future.

A LAST WORD.

I have introduced the reader to a phase of human life which is bound to disappear before the inroads of Western intercourse and civilisation. The empire may crumble to pieces, but the Chinaman himself will retain his vitality, and is a force that the world must reckon with. He is not formidable with the rifle, but is invincible with the spade, and a very good man at the ledger. Left to himself, there is no reason why he should not have gone on for another thousand years as he has done in the past. His civilisation is complete of its kind ; he has gone as far as his principles will carry him. But we have not left him alone, and will not leave him alone, and my conviction is that we shall in the end be swamped by Chinese cheap labour, unless we raise him to our own level. What he most of all needs is a wider, a deeper, and a truer morality and religion. The attempt to impart this is so often pronounced to be a failure that I may record my unprejudiced opinion, based on a good many years' experience as a missionary. It is slow work, and disappointing many a time, but looking at the broad results, they are greater than could have been reasonably expected under all the difficulties. They are not to be measured by a monetary standard, but taken even upon such a basis, they are greater than those obtained by a similar expenditure at home. With all our churches, many people tell us that Britain is going from bad to worse, and yet they hold up their hands in amazement because 350,000,000 of heathen Chinese are not converted by a handful of missionaries, each with a parish as big as a dozen counties, in a few years. "There never was a good work done without much trouble." The Prayer Book in Chinese is a queer compound, and the Shorter Catechism is unintelligible. Jesuit missions became moribund the day it appeared a native convert must become a Papist as well as a good Christian. The Chinaman has no objection to honest cloth from any merchant, but he makes his jacket in his own fashion.

THE END.